T0160969

Praise for *An Archive of Brightness*

"A beautifully shaped, poetic book. Socha's writing is witty but never shallow, with a crow's eye for detail and an archivist's eye for the unexpected meanings that come to the surface of a story when you shake it. She is bold, unpredictable, and a writer to watch."

—Isaac Fellman, author of Lambda Literary
Award–winning novel *The Breath of the Sun*

"The perfect hurricane of rich folklore. Socha has woven together a lawless assortment of experiences, telling a story of queerness, mundanity, and a murder (of crows)."

—Matthew Vesely, author of
Elegy for the Undead

"Socha's intimate and sharp-witted musings give staying power to the ephemera of our individual and collective experiences. As sincerely human as it is philosophical, *An Archive of Brightness* brings insight and depth to the small details of life that are only disguised as ordinary."

—Caitlin Chung, author of *Ship of Fates*

AN
ARCHIVE
OF BRIGHTNESS

AN
ARCHIVE
OF BRIGHTNESS

Kelsey Socha

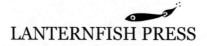

LANTERNFISH PRESS

PHILADELPHIA

AN ARCHIVE OF BRIGHTNESS
Copyright © 2022 by Kelsey Socha

Lanternfish Press
21 South 11th Street, Suite 404
Philadelphia, PA 19107

lanternfishpress.com

Cover Design: Kimberly Glyder
Cover images under license from Shutterstock.com and Juan Lopez /
Addictive Creative / Offset.com.

Printed in the United States of America.
26 25 24 23 22   1 2 3 4 5

Library of Congress Control Number: 2021944927
Print ISBN: 978-1-941360-65-1
Digital ISBN: 978-1-941360-66-8

For Madison
and also for all of the seagulls in Allston

I. *The Middle of the Beginning*

TWO BIRDS ARE SITTING ON A TELEPHONE WIRE, because that's how it goes. The birds are always on telephone wires. You don't get it, but there they are. The birds are crows.

The first crow looks at the other crow and says, fancy meeting you here, and the second crow just looks. It's crows, though, so there can't just be two. Soon they're joined by their whole family tree.

It's night, and it's snowing, and the first two crows just wanted to talk privately, but now Cousin Jesse is here and he's talking about the hockey game, I mean, have you seen those fuckin' seagulls circling the stadium? He keeps going on, explaining to everyone his strategy for getting to the best trash cans, intimidating the ever-present gulls. The first crows move to another tree and try to have meaningful eye contact. But soon the rest have followed them, because that's what it's like to be a crow. You have to be a murder.

Two other crows fly away to a streetlight and caw to one another quietly.

CROW THREE: We have about two minutes before the others follow.

CROW FOUR: So anyway, the moon—

Crow Three nods and opens her beak to answer and then, yet again, a swarm of feathers engulfs them. Crows are patient, but this is a little much.

The crows fly from tree to tree, calling out to each other in the darkness. There are no stars but you can see their silhouettes, bright shapes against a cloudy night sky.

Then the clouds part, and suddenly: the moon. Even though it's snowing, even with the crows.

Crow Four looks at Crow Three and says, I told you. Crow Four closes his eyes and makes a wish. Meanwhile, Cousin Jesse is cawing about the hockey game again, did ya see that giant puffin wandering the stands? Of course it wasn't a real puffin, nothing interesting like that, just a person in a mascot suit, and anyway they don't let crows into the stadiums.

The crows assemble, hold a parliament even though they aren't owls. Have to discuss what there is to be done. The first pair of crows from before finally sneak off to a different telephone wire, shoo away some smug-looking seagulls.

It's no good, says the first crow. It'll never work.

The second crow is silent, sidestepping on the wire like a person with a secret. Spies do this, but these crows aren't spies.

I have been thinking, says the second crow finally. I don't know where this is going. They sidestep some more.

The first crow pauses. We've got to be patient.

They look over towards the crow parliament, shrug. Fly back, wings black against the snow.

Two lobstermen sit in a boat before sunrise. They're looking at each other and shivering in the cold. They haven't caught lobsters in any of their traps yet, and they're over halfway through.

So, says the first lobsterman finally, why doesn't the lobster learn to share?

Why, Tom? says the second lobsterman, sighing quietly.

Tom ignores the sighing.

Because he's a selfish shellfish, he says, guffawing.

The second lobsterman, whose name is Paul, manages a small smile. Across the water, everything is quiet. Water is seeping into the boat, but just a little, not enough to sink it or cause undue concern. In the sky, you can still see a few stars.

Tom is opening the lobster traps now, and he's got one. Shaky antennae and angry claws until he bands them. This is just the beginning, he says.

Paul nods, strokes the lobster's spine, steers the boat to the next location. Tom is drinking coffee from a big thermos, trying to tell more lobster jokes, his voice echoing across the ocean. The ocean looks empty, but Paul knows there are more lobstermen just out of sight, checking their own mess of traps. Nothing is ever as isolated as it feels on the surface.

Paul is in love with Tom and waiting for him to figure it out. Tom hasn't figured it out yet, but he has retrieved another three lobsters in the interim. Paul is looking at him in his knit cap, is looking at him in his stupid rubber boots, is looking at him with three days' worth of stubble he hasn't yet shaved, is hearing his laugh that is probably waking up every fish under the water and scaring away all the crustaceans, and he is thinking, here is a place that I can stay.

Lobster fishing isn't that place, of course; it isn't a place at all. Tom does construction work during the day, and so does Paul when he's not working at the hardware store or helping his mom with errands. You have to do more than one thing to survive, particularly as a lobsterman.

Paul has liked the term *lobsterman* since he first heard it, as if you could be both: lobster and man, a duality. Tom hasn't really thought about it, but he likes to be on the water, and he likes checking the traps, and he likes the lobsters themselves with their many armored legs and big claws and beady eyes, their antennae twitching curiously.

Not enough not to eat them, of course, as he says with a laugh every time he talks about job satisfaction. Lobsters are expensive. Tom hasn't had one in months.

The lobsters newly retrieved from the traps, foiled by salted herring, huddle together in their buckets. They're talking to each other, but the lobstermen can't hear.

The lobsters know that the future was meant to entail flexing their claws, crushing things, exploring. Just now, there's nothing to be done about it. They look up, up, up and see the mostly dark sky, the silhouettes of birds caw-cawing around.

Paul sighs and looks at Tom.

So. You ever hear the one about the lobstermen who fell in love?

Tom doesn't hear him. His hat is pulled way down over his ears and his hearing's been bad ever since the days of Motley Crue concerts, the ones he drove all the way to Boston for and then spent the night slamming his body into other people's bodies, living for the joy of it.

What? says Tom.

Never mind, says Paul. Did you see those birds?

The crows, who have been gathering again for their parliament, are swarming overhead.

Tom, who is not the sort of person to wonder if anything means anything deep down, sighs and wonders if the crows ought to mean anything. Paul, who believes in signs, is already pretty sure they are some kind of omen. The lobstermen lapse back into silence but for the occasional splash of the boat moving across the waves, the crows' wings flapping overhead.

Paul grabs Tom's hand suddenly. They're both wearing gloves. Tom doesn't say anything but lets him keep holding his hand. Paul squeezes, and Tom squeezes back. It's a moment.

The lobsters sigh, but not in awe at the romance unfolding. They're sighing at the sun; it's finally rising.

The lobsters have never seen the sun, not really. Not out of the water. They might not see it again after today. Tom and Paul see it nearly every day, unless it's cloudy.

We all live very different lives.

The lobstermen are still holding hands. Tom turns to Paul. So, he begins.

Paul's heart rises in his chest in anticipation, ready after all this time.

So, why did the lobster think it was so funny to be eaten?

Paul shrugs, says, I don't know, Tom. Tries to play it cool.

Tom grins. He says, Because it just cracks him up. He lets go of Paul's hand to slap his knee and says, Well, that was a knee slapper, and then they are kissing as the sun is rising.

From above, the crows record this event in their chronicle.

None of the crows has ever gone to the cataloging academy, but they've sat on the branches of trees around the academy for a while now, so they feel pretty prepared to build their own archive.

One crow asks another crow, What to do, oh, what to do with all the ephemera?

And the other crow stares at it for a long time, the heap of ephemera, and sighs.

Make sense of it. We have to get more meaning out of it.

Maybe the crows have been spending too much time with humans. Not everything has meaning, certainly not "more" meaning. But crows, they like categorizing.

The first thing, the head crow says seriously, is to find a place to keep our archive. So the crows fly to the secret place, the place in the rocks, the place where they've never seen a human but only other birds. They look around and they say, This will do.

The archive of brightness, one crow says, that's what we'll call it. The other crows privately think it's a bit sappy, but they're too polite to say anything. They sweep the place in the rocks with their feathers. They start scratching into the rock with their beaks, transcribing what they've observed. This is just the beginning.

CROW TWO: But what is it about?
CROW ONE: Something different than what it is.
CROW TWO: What's the difference?

Crow One is busy transcribing.

We need a place to keep these things safe, she says, finally. We'll get to what it's about later.

Crow Two flexes their talons, cocks their head.

Isn't it interesting, they say, how at the end of the world, no one is ever standing in broad sunlight? The world always ends with good lighting.

Are you sure, says Crow One, that you aren't romanticizing the end of the world?

In Antarctica, the only people are scientists or chefs or researchers, and the penguins wander free. The geographic South Pole is different from the magnetic one. Everything is somehow different from what you imagined. Right now, the scientists are waking up and making coffee, and putting on bathrobes. They're not drawing the blinds. Why would you draw the blinds when no one exists to see you?

There are times in Antarctica where the sun doesn't set and one endless day keeps going on and on. Even so, you have to sleep.

Some other times, you have to do the other thing, the thing where there's no light at all and it's always dark. The penguins don't care, but the scientists care, looking more and more tired and clinging to their heat lamps and electric light. The chefs feel similarly, but no one ever talks about them with their too-cold hands, shivering in the artificially bright kitchens. It's all about who's special, the scientists with their glasses and lab coats that they wear even when there's no one else there to see them.

Here is a secret: In Antarctica, everyone's memories get projected outside on the endless white snow. The scientists gather around the windows to watch, to ooh and aww at everyone's first kisses, last haunted houses, or bike riding exploits. It's weird how it works, this memory projector that the scientists invented, but they would explain that memories are collective and you just have to tap in slightly past the surface. Maybe it's not for the best, living in Antarctica, but look—there's a puppy, learning how to walk. It's so big against the snow; nothing we do elsewhere will ever be that vast. Remember this for later: In places that are more or less than Antarctica, things are less connected.

But what, you might be thinking, is the point of projecting memories? Couldn't it make things awkward? What if, say, Lena's memory of sleeping with Jonathan's wife is projected, and Jonathan didn't want to know that, certainly didn't know it regardless of wanting, and now they are stranded together in the snow with bad feelings, and Jonathan wants to put mouse droppings in Lena's coffee but there aren't any mice in Antarctica, so he gets angrier and angrier and walks out in the snow one day and doesn't come back?

Life is full of regrets. Maybe Jonathan made an igloo out of some of the endless snow but we can't see it in the dark, or maybe he didn't; maybe coworkers shouldn't sleep with each other's wives, but also maybe something bad would have happened regardless of where they were. These things have a way of coming to light. At least on Antarctica, there aren't any guns (they were banned by special scientist law after an Incident many years ago).

So far, no memory like that has been projected. Lena probably doesn't even know Jonathan's wife. The scientists haven't had to deal with great betrayals so much as embarrassing memories of nakedness and pink bathrooms and paintings on ceilings.

You ask, of course, if we have been documenting these memories too, and the answer is: naturally, yes, as best we can. Nothing can be allowed to be ephemeral, even on Antarctica. If we stuck with the temporary, maybe we would not remember anything, because the days would blur into one. Almost everyone here stopped writing diary entries a long time ago. They wonder: Do years still mean the same?

An assistant chef keeps a diary, but she keeps it secretly. She keeps it under her pillow and maybe also in her heart, but of course that's only a memory. Or a metaphor. I get these things confused.

In her diary, she writes about the scientist that she's fallen in love with. Lena, of course; it's always Lena. Lena has bright blue eyes and is always doing something to be noticed, like telling stories or baking bread, and the assistant chef has been watching in the way that you do over time, at first casually and then resignedly, and then at long last every gesture starts to look like a sign, every gesture starts to look like it's done just for her. The chef would grow flowers for Lena if she could, but she can't, of course. Nothing grows in Antarctica. Everything's dead or dying or frozen. A better way to phrase it: Everything is waiting to grow, which it might if it ever gets out of Antarctica, but mostly, aside from the people, nothing will.

The assistant chef embroiders hearts onto the inside of Lena's lab coats, but in tiny stitches so she can't see. They're not the cut-out hearts of a valentine; rather, they're anatomical, because this feels more true. She thinks that Lena would appreciate it if she knew—having the genuine article rather than the symbol—but what does she know?

Handmade things are protection. That's the thing the assistant chef knows. If she puts enough care into every invisible stitch, then Lena will be safe, and won't go out in the snow, and the vehicles won't break down, and the sunlight lamps won't fail, and everything will be enough. After a few months of this, of the frenetic sewing—

Where is she even getting ahold of these lab coats? you might ask. In Antarctica, everyone does a lot of things. The assistant chef also does the official Antarctica scientist laundry, so when she irons things and thinks about colors other than white, she holds onto them. We mean she tries to make them new again, better somehow. We've already said this, but handmade things have strange power. They're important, probably.

Anyway, after several months, Lena starts to take notice of the anatomical hearts so small you could mistake them for polka dots or little mendings. Of course they aren't that at all, they're lengths and lengths of love.

Scientists are not that observant of their everyday surroundings, particularly in the snow, particularly when everything around them is white, but Lena notices all the same, eventually. First she feels the small stitching and then she thinks about it and then she gets distracted by global warming and we sit with that for a while, the world slowly/quickly getting warmer, and it's quiet, the thought of this.

Then she remembers, and her magnifying glass is already out so she squints through it, looking closer and closer, and finally she sees it. It's not perfect. Even with all that care, the assistant chef didn't quite get the ventricles right. We mean: This heart would function, but it would collapse under the strain of existence a little quicker than everything else. Still, for embroidery, it's pretty good.

Lena starts to wonder.

As already stated, scientists are not the most observant people when it comes to the everyday. Lena does in fact know Jonathan's wife, who is back in Chile and not here in Antarctica, and was a bit hung up on her for a while. They never slept together, but Lena always admired her perfect hands and exquisite grammar. They got drinks once or twice and discussed linguistics. If Lena were a poet, she would have written poems about her, but as a scientist she's been too busy with the blinding white.

Amid the wondering is this weird bright glow, a flash of something just below her chest, something in the center of her spine, but it's not her spine. It grows bigger every day, so everything seems like it's cast in sunlight (a weather pattern that does sometimes happen in Antarctica, where everything reflects, everything is burning, everything is nothing short of glaring) but right now it's night all the time, which makes the brightness alien. It's like she has a secret, or is wearing the wrong day of the week's underwear—she is suddenly hyperaware of every detail. It's that kind of glow that if you talked about it, you might ruin or crush it, and so Lena stays quiet, playing at the hearts on her lab coat with a faint smile, with this glowing bird inside her chest, just out of sight.

The assistant chef notices the change but doesn't notice the fingerprints on the hearts. It's hard to see things that are right in front of you. She thinks the change in Lena must be due to something else. All she does with her diary these days is color it in, so every day the pages get blacker. The absence of the sun is like this, darker than darkness. But the space just under her chest is glowing too, black and feathered. When she sleeps, she dreams of rolling waves that keep coming; they're over her head, but she is still breathing.

Lena meanwhile stops washing her main lab coat, wears it all the time in case this precious secret isn't made for her and the mistake will be found out if she takes it off. She's getting clingy, which is fair. There's very little else to hold onto in the endless night. Stars, maybe. The moon, sometimes, which could be mistaken for the sun, given enough days in the winter shadow.

Can you see the moon on Antarctica? We sure hope so.

Look: Some penguins are walking along in the dark, doing penguin things. They look at the moon, but they're penguins, so they don't think of it as the moon so much as they enjoy the illumination. It's that simple for penguins, probably.

Back to the story at hand.

Lena won't let go of her lab coat, which is at this point completely covered in hearts, all slightly weakened but still thriving. The assistant chef notices this but doesn't know what it means. Lena's not letting go of the lab coat, and the chef can't iron it, can't stitch more atria on it, more spaces where the love might go, and so she is getting worried. What if the embroidery's charm wears off?

The scientists mostly do their own laundry apart from the lab coats, so there are no other articles the chef can inscribe with protection. She worries and frets and sits on her hands, and eventually starts baking more and bringing baked goods to the labs, just casually. *Protection against winter,* she says as a joke, trying to inspect each coat. Her hands are fluttering and the black bird in her ribs, it's fluttering too. What if it isn't enough?

Meanwhile, Lena is dreaming, looking every day at the hearts on her lab coat with her microscope as if they'll change in the interim, so much so that she's forgetting things. She's getting sloppy. The bird in her chest is fluttering but it's tired.

Once in Vermont, land of no summer, we climbed a fence into the nearby graveyard on a whim, so that we could drink blue slushies among the gravestones. You ripped your tights. Later, we found an entrance that wasn't a fence, but the damage was already done.

Sitting on a grave, we let our hands touch, not looking at each other. You thought it was an accident still, our fingers barely brushing.

In the graveyard, we made a rubbing of a child's grave with wax, which we had on hand. Something about angels and sailors, something about grief, all invisible until we made the rubbing and revealed the secret. Later, much later, you safety-pinned it to your curtain. You held it close.

The moon followed us, we thought later—after the damage was already done. We sat suddenly, quietly, on the bridge that led from your house to the supermarket. We scraped unwanted cake from a party into the river and then sat, hands and knees touching, surrounded by people but feeling alone, the river rushing all around us. We looked up and something looked back. We sat on your car, all touch, all space, and looked up, and something looked back, and suddenly, you thought something like, Oh. Oh no.

Lovers do the looking, or looking makes something into love.

It's hard to write this directly. Let me skip to a different story.

You're dreaming, and the dreams are of radio static, white fuzz on the television. It's nothing clear, nothing to write home about, but you wake up sweating.

You don't remember anything except static, but you know the feeling you had in the dream. It's the usual one, the one where you can sense she is there but hidden just below the surface. Beneath the static, you're together, secret agents meeting under the cover of grey pixels, but secretly, darling, quietly, my dear, always meeting and re-meeting. You can feel her fingertips, but you can't see her.

When you wake up, you're aware of your bones, your hips, your rib cage. Your fingers have been shrinking, and you're wondering if you've lost weight again. It's not that you need to, not that you've even been thinking about it in any serious way, but isn't less always better?

Closer to bones, closer to God, you think, which is a phrase that no one in your life has ever said, certainly not to you—but you like it, so you keep repeating it in your brain. You touch the bones jutting out. You're imagining someone else touching you—how they'll be amazed by the parts of your body that are so delicate, the strange elements of spider monkey and bird. Wings aflutter. You do not have to be good, you think at first, but of course you do. Be better. Be the best.

Be something.

The seagulls are flying outside your window again, but you can't hear a sound. You never hear them make any sort of sound. You try not to mind this but can't help wondering if maybe they talk to other people, the people they like more. They never talk to you, anyway, and the sky, which is vast, never feels like there's anything hidden behind it. You never dream of the sky anymore.

Two crows sit on the grass. Really, a murder of crows sits on the grass, but we're only looking at two, who are looking at something just off screen. One crow nudges the other with a wing.

> CROW ONE: Are we at the interesting part of the story
>   yet?
> CROW TWO: Hush, we're just beginning.

The crows sit in silence for a while.

All parts of the story are uninteresting when you don't have a reason to care. Who determines what pieces of a story get retold?

Around them, other crows are brooding, flapping their wings speculatively, biding their time and wondering if anyone will refer to them, accidentally, as ravens.

The difference between a raven and a crow is whether you're wearing your glasses, or what you instinctually know. Even then, it's a matter of opinion.

Well—says Crow One, but Crow Two hushes her, puts a protective wing around her shoulder.

I am listening, says Crow Two, but they aren't, not really. A feather falls from their wing to the grass. Fluffy feather. Wet grass, wet with dew. The sunlight's hitting the feather but it just makes it look blue. Weird, how sunlight works. Weird how anything works.

> CROW ONE: We remember things. That's what we do.
> CROW TWO (WITH GREAT PATIENCE): Yes.
> CROW ONE: We hold the feelings in them.
> CROW TWO: Now you're getting it.

There's a long pause, and then the first pair of crows takes flight, and then another, and suddenly they're all in the air, then in the trees; everything is giddy anticipation, and then it's quiet again.

A crow's been found dead in the snow. It might be because of the cold. No one knows any reason why they'd be sick, or if it's something to worry about. Sometimes the people who put food in dumpsters poison it, so maybe it's that, but probably not. The crows haven't seen anyone doing that, not lately, and they figure that they would have noticed. Poison is one of those things that crows know deep in their bones.

It's a very old story. It's a very new story.

The crows settle back and wait for the problem to unravel itself. They find something shiny in the snow and follow it. Even when the shine hurts their eyes, they're still watching.

I still don't want to write this directly. Let me try a different way.

Two girls sit on a bench by a waterfall in the middle of Vermont, holding hands, hoping that no one else will see. The two girls, they're blushing.

It doesn't end up mattering in the end, or at least—the ways in which it matters don't matter. The things that you will later wish you had said—these also don't matter, eventually. Put them down.

You were listening to a radio program in the unbearable heat and the light was streaming in through the curtains, and suddenly the radio program was talking about light too, and she looked at you. You burned your hand in the looking and didn't mind or stop.

Honestly, it doesn't matter now. Put it down.

The last morning together, when you thought things would still be okay even if she was leaving, even if everything was about to change—you have to put this down too. The promises, put them down. You have to be able to change your promises.

Love is heartbreaking sometimes, and it doesn't always work. Change your promises.

You had a dream, and when you woke up, she was there talking, but she wasn't awake yet. You let yourself fall in love with this version, the one where the sun was always rising and you were always nestled in the aperture between sleeping and awake, the moments between action. This is the one where you memorized that new alphabet of her asleep on the pillow, trying to trick you into letting her stay in bed. Sometimes you were memorizing the alphabet when you were both awake: the time your house ran out of gas and the burners didn't work so it was cold, suddenly, in the kitchen. No one else was up yet. There was a dead mouse in the mousetrap that she wouldn't let you see, but she saw it. She hid it underneath a towel to keep you safe. You felt lucky.

By the waterfall, you're holding hands, and you're mesmer-ized by her face, but you're worried that you'll see someone you know and that they'll see—not that you're embarrassed, just that it's something small and quiet and new, but of course every-one's already seen and nobody cares. There's nothing to worry about but there's still the imprint of old cares left underneath, still the empty space.

You've been saying that you don't want love unless it's transformative, and, well, that's true, but really you don't want any sort of transformation unless you can control it wholly. So it's not a transformation at all, it's just you and her in the same place, by the same river near the same mountain, a near-endless supply of lives. You are so happy in this future, and you can see it when you close your eyes just right. It doesn't exist, but you can still imagine it.

Did it really happen if no crows were around to witness it? Crow One wonders.

Crow Two shushes her. I was there, they say. I was watching.

Was it worth it? Crow One asks.

Crow Two sighs. It's not over yet.

They both fly away. You can barely see them against the moon.

Two girls sit in a gazebo in the dark, kissing. All their friends are looking for them but they won't find them yet. Two girls are naked in the back of a car, limbs all over, moonlight streaming in. Cramped space, brightness all around.

Two girls are in a parking lot in the middle of nowhere, in a field near the country highway. Two girls are on a hillside, driving upwards, and everything around them is mist, and one of them thinks they might get lost, but there's a full moon and it follows them. Two girls are sitting on a rusted porch swing. They're on a mountain. They're sharing a small bed. The moonlight is streaming in through the curtained window. They're undressing like it's the very first time in the bright glow, the door locked behind them.

In the later but not quite the after, her voice is scratchier, and she calls you nearly every day, a sudden panic each time the phone rings. You are afraid to go to sleep and miss a call. You decide.

What do you decide?

You never look at the moon anymore.

A girl we haven't met yet wakes up one day, notices that she has started to grow wings.

The light's streaming through the windows, and all around her are blankets, but the t-shirt she wore to sleep is ripped now, right around the shoulder blades. There are nubs on her back, and when she touches them, she feels the sharp protrusion of feathers, the stickiness of old blood. It hurts, absentmindedly, like an old bruise.

She goes back to sleep, but when she wakes up, there's still light streaming, still feathers, still that absentminded pain.

She throws on a thick sweater and goes outside, stands on a bridge over the highway, looks up at the light.

People are always standing on bridges, looking at the lights.

She stretches and the nubs of wings stretch too. She looks around, but no one's noticed.

Nearby, a pigeon flies over to her, looks up. And then several more. Pigeons are like crows, never alone.

The girl goes home, gets back under covers. Doesn't get up again until the light stops coming in. Even then, it's a precarious awakeness. She rubs the feathers, pulls, tries to break them, rip them out. It hurts. She can feel blood trickling down her back and winces with the sudden pain.

Outside her windows, the birds are calling out to each other, flying up from the branches, shaking off leaves.

Two crows are watching from the top branch, but she can't see them.

Birds sleeping in her head, birds sleeping in her fingertips, feathers under all this skin. What to do with so much flight?

She goes back to sleep.

In the end of the world that exists in the desert, people are building houses out of scorpion bones. They are waking up and building, and it looks weird, these heaps of exoskeletons, but at least they're doing something, right?

This is what you do in the desert. Things get very strange. Procedures have nothing to be outlined against. It's easy to play to the end. (Maybe don't play to the end.)

The only birds left in the desert at the end of the world are vultures. The vultures write about the scorpion houses in their diaries, in between moments of circling. Huge wings. Feather pens.

One of the house-builders says to herself, what I really need is a man who drinks black coffee. I mean, what I really need is that kind of carpenter. In her head, she has this dream that a handsome, black-coffee-drinking woodworker will sweep her off her feet right there in the middle of the desert, in or out of her scorpion house, which looks like all the other scorpion houses, which is to say shiny and ominous and a bit like death. It reflects the light. Maybe it'll call him to her. She doesn't even like coffee, but she drinks it anyway for the look of it, for the feeling of warmth spreading through her hands when she holds it.

There's a scorpion-exoskeleton coffee shop in town, and it's great if you can get past the crunch of shells underfoot. They've used some of the tumbleweeds as cushions. The desert is a lot of making the best of what you have.

Dreams are like this, you know, sort of impractical, and so the house-builder goes on for a while, drinking her coffee and waking up and going to sleep and spending time with the other inhabitants of scorpion town, and they love their dead houses that were once something else, and they love their coffee and they love each other, but there's always this dream that keeps going on in the background. It will not let any of them rest, the hum of it constantly whining, a sound that no one can ignore for too long.

(There's a montage here, and it's just a woman's hands holding a coffee cup or maybe two coffee cups, but let's not get ahead of ourselves. She's holding one or two coffee cups, and the coffee cups move and the hands are slowly aging—which is the thing about hands, you can't hide the aging, it goes on in spite of you—on and on and on, and then, all at once, the montage ends.)

New scene: The coffee shop owner's sister comes into town, sets up shop.

She doesn't even like coffee, Darryl (the coffee shop owner) says, mournfully, slinging coffee with an air of despondency. And it's true. She comes into town and trips over her own feet, comes into town and laughs too loud, gets scared by the scorpions, gets lost in the desert, only drinks hot chocolate (in the desert of all places), and the house-builder hates her for it from day one.

She's thinking: You talk too loud. She's thinking: The scorpions aren't creepy or frightening, and screw you for coming here if you think that. She's thinking a cacophony of things. She's fueled by hate and wondering when her black-coffee-drinking gentleman caller will show up on the scene. One day, in a haze, she finds the woman who doesn't drink coffee sitting on a pile of tumbleweed looking at the horizon, over a near-endless sea of sand and petrified wood.

The house-builder sits down and they talk, and at first it's obnoxious and deafening, but then the coffee shop owner's sister says something smart about how the sky looks different here, how it's endless in a way that it isn't back in the Midwest, how the vast quiet openness feels bigger and holier and somehow more threatening in the drylands, whereas back home it would have been interspersed with cornfields or big-box grocery store parking lots, sure signs of human intervention that are fully absent here, and the house-builder relaxes just a little bit.

Do you want to come over? the woman who doesn't drink coffee asks, and the other woman, the house-builder, surprises herself and says yes. Then they're in her house, and it has stupid posters, and it isn't made of scorpions somehow (why would anyone make a house without using scorpions?) and it's all very different and smells like pepper and thyme. The woman who doesn't drink coffee is showing the house-builder around nervously, like she's trying to impress her, but why would she be doing that? The house-builder tries to pretend that she likes the decorations, likes the lack of curtains letting the relentless sun inside, how it isn't even dark in here. The house-builder kneads a pillow nervously and doesn't look directly at the woman who doesn't drink coffee, and then all at once they're looking, and then there's a pause, a skip of the record, and suddenly they're kissing and this is unexpected too.

Through the lack of curtains, a vulture glimpses the first kiss, goes home to write it in his diary using a loose feather. He's molting. He's been waiting for something unexpected to change in the desert at the end of the world, has been waiting for a while, and he wonders if this is it.

All the big changes in the desert are recorded in the vultures' book of time. Sometimes the crows consult it, when people move and they want to know the endings. Or the beginnings. Or the middles.

II. *The Beginning of the End*

CROW ONE: Not much good in beginnings.

CROW TWO: I think you mean middles, but look, the middle is where things are growing.

CROW ONE: But what if I don't want anything to grow?

CROW TWO IS SILENT, uses a talon to sort through the vultures' book of time, which is inside a mountain of rock, which is terribly far away from home.

I think there's a pattern here, they say finally, and a vulture hidden in the corner nods solemnly. Crow One has flown away, is somewhere else entirely.

The vulture in the corner is wondering if it's a good pattern or a bad pattern or a different pattern altogether, and what does it mean and how can they make it better? But these are the big, painful sorts of questions that no one ever wants to answer.

The birds have been collecting human stories for years. Honestly, some are terrible, but they are all bound together with visible and invisible threads that run through, connecting points of light. People think that crows are only attracted to shiny objects, but that's not quite true. It isn't just jewelry and foil and precious metals. Often it is these bursts of light.

The birds are hoping that if they can hold onto them, they can make sense of the stories.

We are back in the desert, and the women are kissing, and all the house-builder can think of is that this is nothing like what she's imagined for herself, nothing at all like a handsome, black-coffee-drinking man. Finally she runs out of the house, out of the town, and stands at the top of a cliff and watches the sunset, clenching some scorpion exoskeletons in her fists. It's picturesque, because they're filming a movie in the desert. If you've been wondering whether she's wearing cowboy boots, the answer is yes. She's wearing cowboy boots as the world darkens around her, and the town doesn't know yet, she thinks, so she's still safe, but eventually they'll notice and then something will change and it will not matter at all if she is ready.

There are no secrets anymore. Not here, not anywhere.

In her scorpionless house across town, the woman who doesn't drink coffee is still sitting, playing with the tassels on one of her throw pillows. The camera zooms in on her hands, playing with the tassels and getting slightly older. The motion doesn't change, but the light does. The motion isn't frantic. She is wearing rings. The rings don't change. Time is passing. And passing and passing and passing and—

Eventually, she lets go of the tassels. There's no light, so we don't really see it, but we know. It's the kind of movie where you know.

Eventually, it might be minutes or hours or years later, she leaves her house and goes to the cliff, but the woman who is a house-builder isn't there anymore, she's on her way to the woman who doesn't drink coffee's house to tell her—

Something. We're adults here. It was just a kiss, or it was much more than a kiss, or it was something else entirely, but the sun is relentless like the heat, and it gets into everything and here we still are at the end of the world, a different end of the world. This end of the world is a cliff, which feels apropos, but who knows, really? What is the end of the end?

Time passes, and more time passes. It is the desert, so we mark the time passing by the way the sand moves. Somewhere else and different, we might have seasons.

Close-up on sand blowing in the wind. Close-up on hands aging while holding a coffee cup (not filled with coffee, never with coffee). Long, panoramic shot of cowboy boots on a cliff, getting dustier and dustier.

A scorpion scuttles across the sand. A live one. A vulture observes.

There's this weird silence. Let's stay in it for a while. Or there's this weird noise. Likewise. It takes a lot of time for things to happen in the desert.

Okay, so you know this particular story by now. Two girls, but they're both scared, the glow from all the moonlight fading. The future is coming, and they've been crying for days now, but they're still scared. Neither one wants to say it.

The two girls, they drive up north to the Kingdom to look at weird art and find some beer. They've got crying hangovers, eyes and throats swollen from the night before. It's not great. One girl's driving, but she's so tired. The other one is biting her lip and staring out the window. She's picking the music. She keeps picking sad songs.

The first brewery is closed, and the next one isn't findable— the part of the map where it should be is missing entirely. They keep going.

They keep driving until they get to the edge of the world, though it doesn't feel much like the edge of anything: woods and fields and no other cars in sight for miles. The girl looking out the window wants to say something that will make everything better, but all the words stick in her throat. She taps her fingers against the window instead, a quiet tattoo.

At the edge of the world, they park on the side of the road, wait a minute to get out of the car.

They passed another graveyard on their way to the edge. They talk about stopping there on the way back, as though this were an ordinary day.

Pause.

Is the story done yet?

The crows are getting impatient.

Crow Two sighs yet again. I don't know when it ends, they say, even though it isn't exactly true.

In any case, it's not over yet.

The girls are holding hands and looking at the sky, which is blue and ordinary. The girls are holding hands and looking at this weird bus, and they get on it and look at weird art, and it is weird and wonderful and horrible. There's still no one else around, not even any other cars that are not rusted over. It's just them.

The girl who didn't drive is afraid that if she lets go of the other girl's hand, she'll lose her and be at the edge of the world alone. If she lets her go, she may never be able to find her way back from the edge. But if she turns to look at the girl who drove, she'll be gone forever.

No one is dead. They're just very far north. Sometimes it feels like the same thing.

Looks like rain, the first girl thinks but doesn't say. It doesn't look like rain, but it feels like it. The clouds are hanging over everything.

They keep holding hands, wander the fields. At the end of the world, everything feels like a secret, but it's nice to hold hands in public. Are they in public, if no one else is there? The field is empty. The sky is grey. The sky is vast and intense and terribly lonely.

At the edge of the world, this place they've found themselves in, there is a cathedral with a dirt floor, and they go to it. Not at first, but eventually, after rooms and rooms of dark sculpture and thick paint, still with no one else around. You have to build up to these things.

They wait a respectful length of time. They go up the stairs to the cathedral at the end of the world, and in it are these giant hands suspended from the ceiling. They tighten their grip on each other.

What kind of cathedral has giant hands?

The human kind. The dirt-floor kind.

It has other things too, but they aren't hands; other shapes, which aren't all human, but some of them are. The two girls are alone. They have been alone plenty of times, but never like this.

They sit down on the bench and one of the girls tries not to cry. Maybe both of them try. Birds chirp outside.

Eventually one girl says, we should leave, and the other one says, maybe. Or neither says it, but the cathedral has had its time. The edge of the world has had its time.

They stay just a bit longer. It's so quiet, this quiet. What to do with love when the world is ending?

One of the girls feels wooden. Glued together.

They look up at the hands. The hands, sightless and vast, don't look down, don't acknowledge their presence at all.

The sound of breathing, heartbeats, wood floors, dust.

The girls leave the cathedral down a narrow, winding stair. It's creaky. They don't let go of each other's hands. In the moment, it feels like this will be enough.

Crow One sighs. The end of the world is endless, she murmurs.

Crow Two flutters their wings. It only feels that way afterwards.

They're still at the end of the world, the girls and the crows, but now it's the graveyard a few miles down the street from the cathedral.

You wouldn't think that the end of the world would have streets, but, well. It's not that the world has to end in suburbia, but sometimes it does. In the graveyard, the girls are sitting on a red picnic blanket holding hands. From far away it looks like they're having a casual graveyard picnic, which would be funny or charming, but instead they're just sitting there crying again. The gravestones, which are old and very faded, are mostly circumstantial.

The girls are wearing summer florals. Their foreheads touch, and their glasses clink, and the crows huddle together and wish they had brought snacks for the outing. The girls wish they'd brought more tissues. Everyone wants something.

The sun isn't setting or rising. It's just there. Nothing is great and nothing is terrible, there are just two people clinging to each other on a picnic blanket where words don't work anymore— sooner than expected. The world is loomingly vast in a different way than it was at the cathedral, and a few cars finally drive by, because the end of the world is not always completely isolated. The cars don't stop. Nothing stops, but eventually there are flies. The girls pack up the blanket and get in the car. Nothing stops, and the graveyard is still there. They sit for a long time.

You think, of course, that if this is love, it will conquer everything, but honestly that isn't how love works. It's not all-powerful, not even transformative, really. You've been thinking about the talking, how it fills in the gaps and silences.

You resolve to do better, to be better, but then you're tired again and the bird in your chest is fluttering and trying to get out. The feathers near your heart keep fluttering. You are terrified.

This is the problem with hearts, and jobs, and wings. They can't be guarded in the darkness. You have to leave them on their own; you can't tuck them into bed and tell them it'll be okay in the morning. You feel the feathers rise up in your throat.

You know this end of the world. You dream about it sometimes. You don't go to it yet. How much of writing is retelling? How much of a story is just the rehashing of older stories?

In the end of the world in your dreams, your ex-girlfriend has bought you a shirt. It's green and plaid, and she's saying she thinks it'll fit you really well. You're the same size. It'd fit her really well. In your dream, you're getting dinner together at the end of a banquet table, and there are other people sitting there, but their faces are blurred out. The walls are exposed brick. There's a deer head, looking at you looking at it.

You dream that she's calling to tell you about her day. Stop.

You're drinking wine. Stop.

You're living in a world where she still calls you, still wants to be in your orbit, but you're dreaming it. It can't be real. Stop.

You hate these dreams the most, because you don't hate them. You just wake up and find a quietness to the morning and a brightness that comes with it. You feel, at these times, hopeful, most of all.

The end of the world is you alone in a bright room. There are birds outside your window, but in this end of the world, they aren't watching.

The end of the world feels like being tired. You don't fall asleep, but you're not really awake either. There's this weird sound in your head and it keeps going. The people downstairs are talking and laughing, and the light from the city comes through your windows and keeps going. The end of the world is this place between sleeping and awake, where everything is dark and feathered. But even at the end of the world, night eventually becomes morning.

You just have to stay awake long enough.

In your dream, you are standing in water now. A pool is filling up, but only your feet are covered. It doesn't feel cold so much as it feels like nothing at all. Like air.

The water is up to your knees.

You don't want to be in this skin, with these hands. You don't want this face, these bruises, this weird posture. Everyone sounds dumb when they talk about love. It could be anyone's perfect eyelashes, anyone's dazzling conversation.

The present and ephemeral are no match for eternity. Eternity will win out. You can play the long game and wait, and we will grow into this or grow out of it, the feeling of wanting to bridge any gap between us or to throw things across the room.

The water is up to your waist. It doesn't really matter. I'm going underwater. You're joining me. Here, no one is really safe. Here, take my hand.

In the lobster boat in Maine, Tom and Paul are still kissing. Everything's foggy on the water. While they've been freezing in the moment, life's been going on around them. The lobsters, trapped in their pail, unable to flex their claws, are lethargic. The crows are busy elsewhere.

Another boat in the distance shatters the early morning silence. Eyes fly open, but slowly, everything in slow motion. The men look at each other.

Well, Paul says.

Well, Tom agrees. Guess we better keep checking the traps. The boat's motor starts, loudly.

We haven't gone back to the desert for a while, because it's dry there. Nothing's growing. It's been giving me nosebleeds.

The vulture has been watching in our absence. He's been writing to the crows, but it takes forever for the crows to get the letters, so everything he says lags a few steps behind what's happening, or it would if anything in the town changed. He wants to write sand, just the word *sand* over and over again, but they wouldn't understand.

Let's tell this story again.

The woman, the house-builder, she's always had a dream of meeting her handsome, black-coffee-drinking man. Dreams don't always come true. Her hands are cracked from years of working with scorpions. She wears a cowboy hat wherever she goes, with a different print from her cowboy boots. There isn't a lot of irony in the desert. There's just endless sun.

She loves it there in the sand, where it is so quiet and she knows everyone and both loves and hates knowing everyone. The coffee shop owner has been one of her best friends since they both moved here, although he knows she doesn't really like coffee. The town veterinarian, Julia, has small hands and talks in a stream of nervous pitter-patter, but she's the best with the horses (yes: there are horses in scorpion town). The family of diviners who live on the hill always find water. It is not in any way perfect, but it is so goddamn safe.

The coffee-drinking man started out as a joke, then became a dream, a *someday I will have this*. Things can get bleak in the desert. It is easier to tell stories than to talk about big unspoken things like loneliness. Too-large feelings that you would prefer to run away from if you could.

There is no irony in the desert, just the house-builder sitting with her feelings and not being able to breathe. Here, outside the desert, we've learned about irony. We can laugh about the impossibility of feeling, the inability to exhale.

The house-builder picks at the calluses on her hands, thinks maybe she'll learn to play guitar, scuffs at the dust. It's every-where, the dust. That's what she noticed first in the house of the woman who doesn't drink coffee. No dust anywhere. How does she manage to make everything so clean? It's enough to make a person nervous. She thinks that if she sits on the cliff long enough, the woman who doesn't drink coffee will find her, or the handsome coffee-drinking man who doesn't exist will find her, or the world will finally end, after all this time. One of these options.

It's always been the end of the world, but the woman who doesn't drink coffee is sitting in her house, playing with a pillow.

Staring straight ahead and thinking of less rugged horizons. She doesn't understand the expectations here.

The world doesn't end yet. No one comes to the cliff except some scorpions, but the sun sets. The house-builder goes home, slowly. She had thought that if she waited—well.

As the sky fades from best denim to black, the woman who doesn't drink coffee leaves her house. She's made a decision. She goes to the cliff. She's just a minute or two late. They've taken different directions. Now she's sitting on the cliff, looking up at the stars, but she's at a different part of the cliff. She doesn't know where anything is yet.

The house-builder goes to the other woman's house, but it's too late. The lights are out. She knocks, but there's no answer, waits but there's no answer, says aloud, I guess she doesn't want to see me—the woman who doesn't drink coffee already spoken of in third person, already distant. She writes her a letter, leaves it under a rock.

The letter just is a pictogram, a drawing of a cliff—really a scrawl that looks like a mountain, or an unfinished heart, or something else, if you squint hard enough.

She doesn't sign it, doesn't feel a need. It will be obvious or it will not. The house-builder goes home and sits on her bed and is quiet for a while in the darkness, the silence punctuated only by the hiss of scorpions in the distance. She keeps her eyes open. She thinks about the soft feel of the woman's lips on her own and how it felt like drowning, which the desert almost never feels like, and how everything was strange now. She thinks about the ongoing night, and how sometime it will be day.

You keep your eyes shut for kissing, the house-builder thinks, but she'd kept her eyes open the whole time so she could see everything, the woman who didn't drink coffee's sudden smile, her sharp intake of breath. Kissing like laughing, like making snow angels, a sudden giddy rush.

It's hard to film people in the dark, so the filmmakers shoot these scenes when it's light out with filters, but you can still tell it's supposed to be night, even with eyes open in the dark that don't want to sleep.

Meanwhile, the woman who doesn't drink coffee is just sitting out at the cliff. She didn't know how cold it would get, and she's shivering out there under the stars. She counts them, all of the ones that she can see. She gets to one thousand eighty-seven before she loses track. She's breathing slowly, evenly. The vulture in the corner is also breathing slowly, evenly, trying to stay awake. Dark feathers in the darkness.

The woman who doesn't drink coffee is not sure how she's supposed to be feeling. Right now: cold. Fingers losing feeling. Surprising. Should be more concerning. There's no moon, so the stars are brighter.

She isn't sure how long she's been waiting or what she's even waiting for. Again, no one in the desert has any sense of irony. Irony is taboo in the desert. Finally she sighs and goes home. The vulture struggles to keep up.

Long pan with the camera. Things are quiet. Most of the people in this end of the world are sleeping or reading books or telling stories to their pets. Scorpions hiss. The wind blows the sand into new patterns. The woman who doesn't drink coffee slowly walks home.

She gets to her doorstep and sees the note sticking out from under a rock, but it's dark and she can't read it till she goes inside. New here, she doesn't understand what the pictogram means, but she suspects the house-builder made it. It has that sort of careful feel. Alone now, in her own house, the woman who doesn't drink coffee makes tea, feels the note, and thinks in a quiet way about what it might mean. If the squiggle means *I hoped you'd be there*, or if it means *Please don't stop for me at any cliffs*, or if it means *I am running away to a place with a different sort of weather and won't speak with you anymore.*

Her heart flutters with what she is choosing to call hope. She wonders if the house-builder knows how to play guitar. The filmmakers are still trying to figure out what kind of movie this is, what kind to make it, when the woman who doesn't drink coffee falls back, gets stung by a scorpion.

She's new in the desert, and we don't know much about her aside from her pillows with tassels, her clean house. The hands, the negative space. She doesn't know yet that the scorpions here aren't poisonous. She's convinced that this scorpion sting means she's dying, that she does't have much time.

Her first thought is to go to the house-builder, and then she thinks that's silly, and then she thinks to hell with whether it's silly, she's dying. Suddenly it's a different kind of movie and she crawls to the house-builder's house, which she recognizes by the scorpion banner out front.

The filmmakers are worried: they don't know for sure about the effects of scorpion stings. They think she'll be fine, but maybe they've bitten off more than they meant to. Much like the scorpions.

The vulture composes his letter to the crows, says, It is a very long night in the desert.

The crows, across the world, nod and cough up sand. (This will happen later.)

You can't knock on the door of a scorpion house, as it doesn't echo enough. She lets herself in. Upstairs, the house-builder is lying on her bed, completely still. In the dark, you can see her freckles. You can imagine them, anyway.

The woman who doesn't drink coffee drags herself into the house but doesn't know where the house-builder is, has never been inside a scorpion house. She winces and whimpers and waits. She thinks, okay, if this is meant to be, if she's meant to save me, she'll know I'm here.

The filmmakers think this is great footage. The vulture worries about the woman's self-preservation instincts.

The house-builder gets up, goes down the stairs, and nearly trips over the woman who doesn't drink coffee, who's curled up on the floor and looks passed out. The house-builder doesn't see what's down there at first, then she does but thinks it's a vision, an apparition, like she's dreaming with her eyes open about the woman who doesn't drink coffee coming to her house. It shouldn't look like this, right? Dreams twist things sometimes.

The woman who doesn't drink coffee lies there. Her eyes suddenly open wide. The bite doesn't hurt as much anymore; she's sure it's because she's about to die. She says, You're here.

The house-builder raises an eyebrow and says, *You're* here. Different inflection. She sits down beside the woman who doesn't drink coffee, sure that she's here to talk about the kiss.

Mentally gears up to say, I'm sorry, but you're not my handsome black-coffee-drinking carpenter. Mentally gears up to say, I don't know what I was thinking in your clean house with all that sunlight where I could barely blink or hide.

She coughs. The dust. It's everywhere.

The woman who doesn't drink coffee whimpers slightly, says, I think I'm dying, which is not what the house-builder expects. Her heart starts to pound. She asks, What's wrong? Sure that the end of the world has finally come to the end of the world, she checks the woman who doesn't drink coffee's pulse. It's faster than average, but not dangerous.

The woman who doesn't drink coffee's eyes flutter shut. Not to be picturesque, but the angles on this shot in the dark are pretty amazing after the terror and the pain and the getting here. The house-builder looks at this woman who might be dying in her house, who has just shown up at her doorstep. Takes the full picture of her in, puts a hand to her forehead.

Light's streaming into the house somehow, even in the darkness, but all of it is blue. It's night and it's beautiful, but the house-builder is no longer focused on secret kissing. She's worried about the potential death happening near her knee-caps. She turns on a lamp, and everything changes. Different glow.

The pulse checked, she looks over the body of the woman who probably isn't dying. Shyly, nervously. This is not the flight from town she's been planning. Really: flight. She was going to call a small plane in the morning, find a different end of the world, possibly a better one.

She looks over the body, which belongs to a person who's still breathing, and can't see much damage. Looks again. This could take hours.

The vulture steps in with a cue card that says, LOOK AT THE ANKLE. The boom operator who's just outside the shot gives him a thumbs up.

The house-builder's heart is pounding. She's not sure where else to look, what to do. But she sees the cue card, finally, looks at the ankle, and sees the place where the scorpion venom has oozed in. Puts her lips to it carefully and sucks the venom out. It's not bitter or deadly, just numbing. She spits it out in the dust. Repeat.

In the background, there's some heartrending Spanish guitar music and tumbleweeds rolling across the desert.

She puts a cold compress on the wound. Applies pressure.

The house-builder looks at the woman who probably isn't dying, checks her pulse again. Shyly, like a new lover. She carries her to the couch, which is made of scorpion, because what isn't made of scorpion here? It's the only building material anyone knows. But it's well-upholstered and unexpectedly soft. She covers the woman who probably isn't dying in a blanket, then sits on the floor next to her. Stands up. Shifts. Paces the floor. Weird starlight streams in through the mostly curtained windows like weird bright feathers.

She moves the head of the woman who probably isn't dying so that it's in her lap. Strokes her hair. Resolves to stand guard all night in case the breathing thieves come.

Who are the breathing thieves? the crows wonder.

When the house-builder was a little girl, her mother used to keep watch over her and her brother, and when they asked why she was there, rather than just appreciating the moment, her mother would look at them very seriously and say, You don't want the breathing thieves to come, do you?

And the house-builder, who quite desperately wanted her mother to stay until she fell asleep but didn't want to admit to it, would shake her head furiously and hide her nose underneath the pale pink covers, hide Peter Bunny too, where they'd both be safe.

The house-builder thought her mother was joking, but once or twice she woke up to see a mirror held to her nose. The breathing thieves haven't come yet, her mother would whisper. You're safe, go back to sleep.

The vulture does not wonder. He knows all of this. He's been watching for a very long time.

The crows cough up the dust they've breathed in during the letter reading.

They don't want to say that it all makes sense now, but at least it's beginning to fit together. Write back soon, they caw.

The woman who probably isn't dying and who doesn't like coffee opens her eyes, surprised to discover that she's still alive, she's not on the floor, and someone is playing with her hair.

She reaches up, feels the house-builder's callused hand, holds it and doesn't let go. Shuts her eyes again.

The house-builder's chest birds are all trying to fly, but she settles for squeezing the hand of the woman who probably isn't dying. In the blue light, these hands are almost beautiful. The vulture in the corner lets his eyes fall shut. The rest can wait until morning, he thinks. We're safe.

The filmmaker says *cut*—doesn't shout it, just says it quietly. Yeah. That's what I wanted, he murmurs. He's getting tired. The desert is taking its toll.

The cameras aren't rolling anymore, but the house-builder and the woman who probably isn't dying keep holding hands. No one turns more lights on. At the end of the world, the night goes on.

In her envenomed sleep, the woman who probably isn't dying dreams about the moon. It's watching her intensely. She can't tell its gender, although she's always thought it was feminine.

The scene changes again and she's back in Indiana, and everything is snowy and flat. She wanders the sidewalks but keeps getting lost. Too much white; it covers her footsteps every time she changes direction. Cars keep crashing at the intersections. Sirens keep wailing. She doesn't recognize anyone. She crosses herself to ward off evil. The sky goes dark.

The scene shifts again, and now she's in the desert, she's in her brother's house, and he says, I'm glad to see you, but I'm not sure why you're here. You don't like dust and you don't like scorpions and you certainly don't like coffee, what are you going to do?

She says, I'm here to see you, but even to her ears it doesn't sound convincing. She tries again, says, I needed to get away, and this sounds more true. He wraps an arm around her shoulders, awkwardly careless, shows her around town, and says, Our house-builder built all of these. Look at the scorpion shells, don't they shine? You'd hardly know they were dead.

The woman shivers. Every town is the end of the world, but she doesn't know this yet, doesn't feel the ending coming yet, just sees the reflective houses. She says, The house-builder's very talented. Where do they keep finding the scorpion shells?

Her brother shrugs. It's the desert. What else are you going to find? Oh man, I can't wait for you to meet her. She always compliments my coffee. She helped me polish my espresso machine, made spare parts out of bone. A woman like that, she's something special.

The sister nods, says, I'm sure she is, but she can't help wondering: What kind of person builds a whole town out of something dead?

Then she's deciding to stay for a while. She's building her house, and it's not made of scorpion at all, and everyone is looking at her funny, like she's doing something wrong, like aluminum and glass aren't reasonable building materials, but she's decided to stay so she ignores them.

In the dark, in her head, the scorpion bricks all over town start moving and hissing, start screaming at her. They've come alive, she thinks, but she's too tired to do anything about it. Fade to black. An uneasy peace.

In the corner, the vulture's wings flap, then go still.

CROW THREE: Is it the end of the world yet?
CROW FOUR: Not quite.

A pause.

CROW THREE: Are they falling into something?

CROW FOUR: Not if I can help it. Let's distract them.

There's a big commotion: bird noises, feathers flying, moments broken.

CROW THREE: Did we stop it?

Another pause.

CROW FOUR: They'll grow into it or out of it. Right now
they're doing neither.

The crows scatter again, pretend to be leaves. It starts snowing. You stop watching the garden, find shelter.

Leave the crows for a minute. Follow a seagull that's circling in the overcast sky, which looks harsh or exciting, depending on your point of view.

You're by the harbor, near where all the ferries go. The end of the road. You stand on a water-taxi ramp. It's empty. At the edge of the water, another seagull preens. It's cold, it's raining, the wind is blowing. Your shoes are getting wet.

The seagulls try to pick fights with gangs of pigeons, many of whom have lost limbs. The bird world can be brutal.

A harbor attendant announces that a ferry to the island is boarding. Foghorns sound in the distance. The rain goes on.

It's hard to sit with uncomfortable things and stay quiet. No one likes that kind of silence.

Meanwhile, in Antarctica, it starts to snow again.

Things in Antarctica are much the same. The scientists look at their phones, check Facebook feeds. Memories are still projected on the snow, but the snow's changing, so the memories are changing too. The grains of snow are smaller this time.

At night, everyone huddles together to watch a special selection of memories. They aren't marked as belonging to a certain person, but you can usually tell whose they are. Most of the memories are from the time before Antarctica. Everyone's always thinking of the past here.

The image shifts to a pair of hands. Stubby fingers. Small scars. Freckles. The hands are touching a lab coat over and over again, feeling something that's invisible against the snow.

Everyone is too polite to say, Well, this is kind of a lame memory. But they're thinking it. The feeling in the room gets impatient. They want to see puppies, they want to see babies, they want to see the ways in which people's lives have been changed irrevocably. The big kinds of love and things other than love, the ones that stand out sharply against the background. What's the good in seeing more white?

In a minute, the slideshow moves on to more interesting sights, thank goodness. Two babies learning to walk and giggling. People falling in love on a train, in the grocery store. A plate being thrown, breaking. Then another. Sudden violence. When you watch your own memories, do you watch them in third person? How close can you get?

The assistant chef is clenching her knuckles so tightly that they go white. She knows the hands that just appeared on the snow. She wonders what to do now, if anything needs to change. The snow keeps falling.

Lena the scientist is rubbing her thumb and index finger over the threads in her lab coat again and again. With enough friction she could wear a hole in the heart. It's already exhausted.

The problem with Antarctica is that we all know the ending and no one likes it. That's why we watch memories in the snow. That's why we obsess over the past. There's irony in Antarctica, but let's be clear: nothing grows here. Nothing can. The continent is starting to thaw, maybe, but it's still a place for investigation, not for change.

The assistant chef desperately wants to keep Lena safe. Lena desperately wants to do good science, to fight off the feeling of being tired. It isn't that they're doomed, just that good luck charms don't always pay off, even with the best of intentions.

The assistant chef goes back to her room and starts knitting a hat, thinking care into every stitch. She starts crying, though, an unfamiliar sensation, and so she stops. Objects can pick up emotions. Everything does. The assistant chef shuts her eyes, falls asleep on her knitting needles. The endless night continues.

Still watching the snow, Lena puts her head in her hands, lets the lab coat go slack.

The snow is still falling. The plates are still breaking. It's exhausting.

The memories are silent. The wind would block out the sound, if there was any, but still.

The assistant chef has been having nightmares. Finally, she dreams of hands. Lena's. Fingers twisting over and through each other, again and again and again. Everything repeats itself in dreams. Dreams think nothing of monotony.

Later, the assistant chef wakes up and goes to work, bakes bread. Thinks about the future. Wonders if she'll leave Antarctica when her contract ends, do something somewhere else with a more jagged skyline. Wonders what Lena's doing in her lab, in her lab coat.

Just then, Lena enters the kitchen, asks if she can help in any way. She's fidgeting. The assistant chef's lungs feel like they're being sat on, a new and perilous sensation, the bird in her rib cage suddenly waking up. She nods, gestures that Lena should knead the second loaf of bread. She's up to her elbows in flour. She can't speak, or at least she won't speak, which is almost the same thing. They knead bread in silence, side by side. Finally, Lena speaks, says, It's nice weather we're having, which the assistant chef thinks is a joke, because the weather is always the same, always snow. But she can't be sure. She nods, smiles slightly.

Silence. Static.

There are other chefs in the kitchen, but not close by. They are background noise. Everything's chrome and white, sterile brightness. Like everything else in Antarctica, the kitchen is starkly practical.

Pots clatter. Snow is falling. The assistant chef is so aware of Lena standing next to her, of the glasses sliding down her nose. She wonders: if she plays dead, goes limp, will Lena stay forever? She keeps her elbows tucked in, tries to focus on the bread.

Lena is trying to resist touching her lab coat, to resist running out of the room and into another one, then out of that room into the ever-falling snow. The bright bird behind her rib cage feels like it's choking.

Finally, Lena speaks again, after an endless, nervous, bread-kneading silence, and it's about Antarctica. What else is there to talk about? You know, the Scott expedition, she begins, and the assistant chef nods quickly. In Antarctica all sorts of things are named after Scott.

I do, the assistant chef says, and Lena nods quickly, acknowledges her and keeps going.

Right, so the Scott expedition—Terra Nova—they were winning against all the other expeditions—and then they got lost in the snow and froze to death. And then the Amundsen expedition—

Lena pauses. Laughs. Says, I swear that there's a point here. They make eye contact. The assistant chef smiles, nods. Keeps kneading, muscles tensing. There are moments, she thinks, where things have to change or stay the same. She wonders about this moment. She tries to pay very close attention to what might happen next. The bird in her chest is flapping nervously.

It's difficult to document a series of events in Antarctica, because penguins do not make good scribes. So the telling can only fall to the birds that live inside the rib cages, these birds that are hardly even representations of birds, just feathers and hope—yet they still have to perform as emissaries.

The assistant chef takes another shallow breath.

The birds in the chests don't even know that it's snowing.

It's too cold for your fingers. They fall off and you think, well, no fingers anymore, guess I can't write, but you can still talk, so you keep going. The night sky is full of tiny stars.

On her couch, holding hands with the woman who probably won't die, at least not anytime soon, the woman who builds houses out of scorpions finally lets her eyes shut. She doesn't dream of anything except sand and dust. It's making patterns, but none of them are clear in the space behind her eyes. The filmmaker goes to sleep in a corner and dreams about falling, which even in his dreams he finds a bit unoriginal, but he keeps stepping off the cliff over and over again anyway.

The crows puzzle over the vulture's letters, wonder what will happen next.

I think there's a pattern, one crow says finally. He signals, tapping his beak.

On the highway, there are no deer, no squirrels, no live animals of any kind. Just cars and trucks, passing each other over and over against a monotonous backdrop of twenty-four-hour gas stations, rest stops, and grassy embankments. At the end of the world, the truck drivers keep driving, and they keep thinking that soon it will be morning, but morning is always a few hours away.

Occasionally you find yourself not at the end of the world but at the beginning. It's frightening and unexpected.

At the beginning of the world, everything is old and new at the same time. It feels like all the other places you've lived, but slightly different. Not better or worse, just different. The colors are the same. The streets are all under construction. You're afraid of the beginning of the world, but you don't want to say it out loud.

The beginning of the world is not Antarctica. It isn't a desert. At the beginning of the world, there are rarely cathedrals. At the beginning of things, no one knows what to pray to or pray for. That comes later.

The crows begin to recount this to each other, but of course they weren't there. There are no crows at the beginning of the world.

How do you know when it's starting? one crow asks, finally.

The other crows are silent.

Not everyone likes birds, Cousin Jesse caws, hesitating.

The other crows caw and whirl around, switching trees in a black haze of feathers.

It's snowing still. The cobblestone streets are slippery. The local team lost their last hockey game, but the crows don't mind. There are few things that the crows mind. We're divided, the crows think. Some of us are leaving, and some of us are left.

They are trying to write a different story. It's hard to know why they might care.

Meanwhile, the girl who is growing feathers is waking up again. The wings are getting bigger. She can't keep hiding them under a backpack or sweater, can't go out, can't even breathe.

It hurts, crushing the feathers, trying to hide them. It aches, this dull constellation of pain, and her room is a million bright points of light. She wonders how long this stage will last. They've been growing for a while, all hollow shaft and black down. They aren't beautiful.

The girl with the feathers has always liked birds, but this was never something she had in mind. Not everyone wants a transformation.

Transformation is not always a choice. This is a thing you learn over time.

It hurts to change. This is another thing that takes time to learn.

The wings have started stretching and flexing of their own accord. The girl pulls the scratchy wool blanket over her head and goes back to sleep surrounded by the light, trying to block it out.

Do the wings sleep?

The birds outside watching know.

At the end of the world that exists only in the north and in memory, two girls are still sitting in a car, staring straight ahead at a graveyard. They aren't quite silent, but they aren't making a lot of sound either. Loud pop music is playing in the background. It's overcast. It's August. Nothing in the world is as red as the picnic blanket they were sitting on earlier.

The girls are still holding hands, and finally one says, I guess we should be leaving, and the other one nods. Things were so funny and bright earlier, but now nothing is funny. It's simply tired, like they're still trying to find their way out of the cathedral's strange shadows.

It's like the lobstermen on their lobster boat—that kind of

not speaking. The car is a vast plain of things left unsaid, tumbleweeds crossing a desert. The drive, the fields, the cathedral, the graveyard—the end of the world is starting to feel like a complete lifetime lived in a single day. No one lets go of anyone's hand—neither is letting go of the other one's hand even now—but what does that mean?

The sky is so gray that it is beginning to be oppressive. I mean that it's stifling, I mean—I wonder if it'll rain, one of the girls says.

The other one shrugs. Transformation is exhausting.

CROW ONE: Are we at the end yet?

Crow Two shakes their head, flaps their wings, flies away in search of more snacks. The two of them are alone, finally. They've snuck away. The other crows are having a meeting.

At the crow parliament, the head crow (it's Cousin Jesse, who has suddenly risen to power in an unexpected election, which had mysterious timing what with all the crow deaths, and the weirdness in the air, and the sudden success of Jesse's favorite hockey team, but anyway—) clears his throat, utters some gentle caws, steps up and down his branch nervously.

There's been another letter from the vulture in the corner, he says, nervously preening.

It isn't that the crows don't like the vulture, but, well, there's the dust. Also his epistles read like film scripts. They make the crows tired.

Well, says Cousin Jesse, head of crow parliament.

He opens the bulging letter with his beak.

All the crows, even the ones that snuck away, all of them sigh in awe. The letter is shining, bright as aluminum foil or lobster pots.

This is, after all, why they collect things.

It's been hard for the vulture, out in the end of the world in the desert. A group of vultures would be a committee, or a kettle, or a wake, but there's just the one, so he's just a vulture. Vulture, Esq., he says sometimes, tiredly, but it's not really funny and doesn't make much sense. He's lonely. He's never much liked scorpions, but he really doesn't like seeing them made into houses, however expertly crafted.

He sounds worried about what will happen next in this story. See, the filmmakers who are shooting it, they're really overrunning the town. It seems like the house-builder and the woman who doesn't like coffee barely notice them, with so much else going on, but the same can't be said of everyone. The filmmakers have been ruining the desert for days with their requests for hot water and their nylon tents. There are chemicals in the breeze that burn the vulture's nose. What, he wonders, will happen when they stop shooting?

Ordinarily, you find out the answer when everything goes dark, but lately the stars have been especially bright. Lately, the lamps have been working especially well. It's always been quiet in the desert at the end of the world. Now it's getting deafening.

The coffee shop in the desert has run out of coffee. What to do? This is an unprecedented event, but with everything happening—

Well, there will be more on Tuesday.

Silence, stretching onward. Film crew's unhappiness, stretching onward. Everything is a stretch.

There's no coffee in the coffee shop—there's not much of anything in the coffee shop—but there are still people in it, and they're still speaking in hushed coffee-shop voices and admiring the scorpion-bone espresso machine. This is the wonderful thing about people, amid untold horrors large and small: at least they are consistent.

They are looking at their hands.

The coffee shop owner is wondering right about now why he hasn't seen his sister in a while. It's been busy, but she's been gone for a while, and usually they'd have had dinner by now. He would cook, and she would bring alcohol, and they'd talk about their parents. This is the way things usually go.

His sister is very quiet in the house-builder's bed. Not moving. Not looking at the scorpion ceiling. Arms wrapped tightly around the house-builder's waist, head on her chest. Eyes shut. It isn't the bad sort of quiet.

The end of the world is sometimes, honestly, a relief.

The house-builder kisses her forehead.

They've been sleeping, mostly, since the woman who probably wasn't going to die realized that she probably wouldn't die. They haven't been talking. Shades drawn. Arms tightly wrapped around each other. This is not what anyone expected.

It's a bit like drowning but in a safe, cozy-feeling way.

At some point, of course, they will have to wake up. The vulture knows this. The women know this. The filmmakers, who have lately been distracted by the lack of coffee and hot water, but will soon be back, know this.

For now: eyes shut. Breathing in unison. Faint smiles. Remember, there's very little irony in the desert.

At the end of the world that exists in the Midwest, the one where it's never August or always August, the feeling of inertia lasts.

In the mornings, the streetwashers clean the streets, and we rise early to see them do it. Everything is peaceful and flat, and there's a soft spray of water on pavement. The sun rises behind the buildings. We want to get to high ground to see it. The best high ground is the parking structure in the center of town, so we go there, climb every flight of stairs to reach the top.

Everything is as it was before. We find it impossibly beautiful, the continuing.

Also, we find it flat. The sunrise is grey.

We know every street by heart, each square. Count them like a counting song that helps you fall asleep at night. Walk them, and walk them, and walk them again.

The end of the world in the Midwest? It's like a dream, not a bad one, but a hazy one. We barely remember it now.

Across the dock, the lobstermen are getting out of their boat. They're selling the lobsters at the fish market and pocketing the cash. They once made a deal to sell lobsters to the Walgreens over near the Trader Joe's, but that was years ago, and they regretted it. Paul says he doesn't think that that's a life for anyone, not even a lobster. Antennae growing long as they wait. Tom agrees but doesn't say it, just lets Paul keep talking.

The lobstermen are taking off their rubber coats, their rubber waders, their rubber galoshes. It's quiet, just the squidge of rubber on rubber. The men aren't saying anything, and then finally:

So, Paul says. He's been gearing up to this for a while.

So, Tom says, after a long pause. How about that hockey game?

Paul nods and busies himself with carefully taking off his gloves, then putting his non-boating coat back on. His convenience-store-clerk coat. The boys are havin' a good season, he offers, and waits.

Tom, he's not saying anything, and it isn't a silence that says, I wish I'd pushed you off the boat to avoid this conversation, just the kind of silence that maybe can't end in any easy way. The crows watch this, amused as well as tired.

What other emotions do crows have?

(Worried, gleeful, scheming, victorious—)

Nothing about this moment is like a movie. In a movie, all the waiting would be leading up to something. A date at a bar, hand-holding in public, a marriage proposal, tiny adopted lobsterman babies, watchdogs, matching rockers.

But it's cold at the end of the world in Maine, the one where time never stops. The world never narrows down to just two men on a lobster boat, while lobsters look on with beady eyestalks thinking they see seagulls. It has a bigger shape than that. Paul has been around a while. He knows you can't will the world into shrinking because you want it to.

Tom's finished changing. He smiles at Paul. Tomorrow then? he asks, and Paul nods, slowly.

There are a few hours a day where the world can be as small as you hope it to be. Most of them are before anyone else wakes up. By mid-morning, it's always a bit bigger than anyone can manage.

A lone seagull calls out as the men walk to their separate cars, carefully not looking at each other.

In the fish market, the lobsters look at each other and think about the sky. They fall asleep with the water of the tank rushing around them. The lobsters have not figured out the world; they don't know it's the beginning of the end. They float in the ever-running water.

The lobsters are waiting for death, but they don't know that either. They just think they're waiting.

Outside, it's raining. The ocean is getting rougher. The crows sigh and go to find the rest of their murder.

III. *The End of the End*

TWO CROWS SIT TOGETHER UNDER A PARK BENCH. One says, Finally, we can be alone.

The other crow nods, wraps a wing around his shoulder.

These are not our crows. These are different crows. Why are they alone?

It's raining. The murder has scattered, trying not to get their feathers wet. The rain on the pavement looks like oil slicks. Under the park bench, this lone pair of crows watches pigeons with thinly veiled resentment. The first crow leans into the other crow's wing.

We need to talk about the end of the world, he says finally. The other crow, the officially elected Jesse, nods. He's been shrinking. Holding so much power has been terrifying.

Together they fly to the water. Look out, here it is, one says.

What? asks the other.

The end, says the first. Pauses. Not of the journey, just—

The world ends here, and it ends here, and it ends here, and it will end here, and by the next full moon it will end here, and in August it will end here, and this is the ending for October, and after a while it won't seem like they're separate worlds, these endings, but they are.

Every story must come to a close. The crows search the water urgently.

This is not the close. This is not the close.

The crows are getting soaked.

You sent me a copied-down love poem in the week before everything ended. It got returned to sender by some weird twist of fate, but I asked and you sent it a second time, even after everything that happened, and then it was mine to reckon with.

We always thought about love differently. Whatever its taxonomy, the feeling has not gone anywhere. Even if the car is gone, the love is old, the story is something to remember in February or in the middle of summer when we are very tired. In the future that isn't coming, we live by a mountain and the world is both very quiet and very loud all of the time.

In the future that has already come, things were predetermined, and then they were not. Leaving isn't the same as not wanting you, not even the same as not choosing you, just a point of divergence.

Your absence is:

A line unconsciously crossed. The line is gone. The floor is gone. No way to find a way back to it.

A poorly constructed thesaurus that doesn't know the new words we've been adding. Nothing like your word-of-the-day app that updates itself.

A great absence. Period, end statement. Once, I believed in you.

The world with you keeps ending. The world without you keeps ending. Nothing about this part ever changes.

The girl who's been growing wings, she's finally decided that enough is enough. She stands on her fire escape. Her shoulder blades flex. The wings flex. She wonders if this is what it feels like to be a bird. She takes a deep breath. She jumps.

The wings, monstrous and painful, begin to flap of their own accord, catching the wind. It's like they belong to someone else, someone more prepared to fly.

She lands, gently, on the street.

The filmmakers have gone almost a week without coffee and they're still sitting listlessly around the coffee shop with their recording equipment and dirty hair, while the woman who doesn't like coffee and the house-builder are telling stories about their childhoods in hushed tones at the scorpion house.

(All the houses are scorpion houses, you might be thinking, but you know which house they're in.)

Everyone else is distracted. No one else has fully noticed that these two are missing amid all the chaos. The woman who doesn't like coffee is now fully recovered from her scorpion mishap, but she still lets the house-builder check her ankles to make sure that they're all right, and the house-builder kisses her ankles and laughs. That is what being in the scorpion house is like right now.

Left alone without cameras, they forget to argue, just look into each other's eyes.

The woman who doesn't like coffee is talking about how when she and her brother were small, they made mud pies in their backyard, and she decorated them with dandelions and tried to get the neighbor kids to eat them, and her brother wandered off and caught a toad and they kept it as a pet until they forgot to give it enough water and then they found it dead outside, and her brother cried and made her do a proper funeral for it. They made a grave marker out of a rock, but their dad ran over it with his lawn mower and the lawn mower made a weird sputtering sound, and he got mad and made them move it.

She pauses. That's what Indiana was like, she says.

The house-builder has never been to Indiana, but she nods. Her cowboy hat casts a shadow on her face.

The other way that Indiana is, says the woman who doesn't like coffee, it's like this. Everyone's nice to your face, and the grass is so green, and everyone goes to the city council meetings and it's fine and everyone talks about how much they love the city and how glad they are to be here, and then after the city council meetings, people go home and kill themselves. No one sees it coming.

It's matter-of-fact and out of the blue, far more than the house-builder was prepared for. The house-builder wonders if this is the kind of thing everyone talks about when they let their guard down. Maybe later, she and the woman who doesn't like coffee will look back and say that this—this was the start of something. (At this point, what they have is nothing but a series of starts, a chart whose stars are forever rising.)

The house-builder wonders if this is what love is like, people in dark houses talking about their scars, their tectonic rifts. If she collects enough painful facts, will they stay together forever? Maybe romance is an encyclopedia of trauma, carefully indexed, with someone else bearing witness.

She doesn't say any of this, merely nods.

And the woman who doesn't like coffee, whose scorpionless house is collecting dust right now in her absence, she nods too without a hint of a smile, clenches her fists, and says, It's a fact. Someone dies after every city council meeting.

(It isn't a fact, but it might be a truth. They're different things.)

Anyway, she sighs, leaning into the house-builder. Tell me about where you're from?

The house-builder wonders if there are things she should be asking about Indiana, important information she should be mining from this conversation. Maybe if she asks the right questions, they'll stay on track.

Through the darkened windows, you can't even tell that it's the middle of the afternoon.

The two girls are sitting on a porch swing looking at fireflies in a field. One girl has never seen fireflies before, somehow.

The other girl is holding her hand through the rusting metal, laughing at how excited she is.

The sun has set, but the sky is so bright you almost wouldn't know it.

Maybe, Crow Two says, maybe this should be the ending.

The archive of brightness has been set up in earnest now. It glimmers. It's a secret city. The crows are entranced and trying to pretend that they're not that committed to it, that it's just a side project.

The archive is organized by time of day, and then geographic location, and then by color. It takes a great deal of practice to understand. Cousin Jesse is still wrapping his beak around it.

In one vault are the vulture's letters, sand and all. Later, the crows will add copies of the filmmaker's tapes, ones that they've stolen while the director wasn't looking. They want to make a definitive collection.

The sun is setting. The birds go to sleep.

Two girls are sitting on a porch swing staring at a field in a place they won't find themselves in again. Irony exists at this end of the world, but it's no less heavy-handed than sincerity. No one can see them on this side of the house. No one can see them if they keep pretending to be shadows.

They're smoking a cigarette, slowly, handing it back and forth. Fingers brushing when they pass it back and forth, lingering. Intentional. It burns in their lungs. It's filtered, so it burns in a filtered way. It's gold, which means light, a perfect smoking ad from when smoking ads were still cool.

Two girls kiss and neither of their mouths tastes like ash. One of the girls is wearing a denim vest. The cigarette box is in her vest pocket.

No one can see her, though, remember? She's a shadow. The other girl, the one who is also a shadow, is playing with her lighter. She bought it after the other girl kept losing hers. Both the cigarettes and the lighter came from the gas station down the road. The man who owns the gas station can see them, but only separately, even when they're together.

The girl holding the lighter is always forgetting that they're separate. Sometimes they go to different places, and it feels like they are each other's phantom limbs. We're orbiting, she said once to the other girl, who nodded. We are planets.

I lied, earlier, when I said that this end of the world had irony. Only one of the girls can feel irony. It's a split ticket.

They aren't planets. They are magnetic fields. The girl in the denim vest is talking. It's a poem she didn't write, but she did copy it down by hand. She has her reading voice on, and it is lovely and scratchy and terrible.

The paint on the side of the house is chipping.

All these events take place before they drive to the cathedral. And they happen after. All this time not letting go of hands, mostly forward-focused. The porch swing doesn't go anywhere except back and forth.

There comes a point in love, or at least in care, where it becomes an excavation. Lovers become archeologists. They dig past the skin to the veins, past the surface to the things that hurt. And past those to the things that hurt more. Getting to know someone dear becomes a series of pain tours, a lesson in gentle disinterring. A hollowing out of cavities.

But after a while, this excavation, it starts to feel like rote, like a script. As familiar as the radiator whistling or the birds outside cawing, a series of small motions that you can already predict, already play to the center. The revealing of small atrocities, the unveiling of insecurities. You learn your script and recite it. Worse, you learn everyone else's.

It gets very tired.

You are underground, and someone who loves you is trying to bring you back up, but they won't look at you. You call out to them but they won't look at you, and you think, why crawl up into the light if this is what it's going to be like. And you think, I'm going to have to have the same conversations all over again.

You call out their name again. They look. You've ruined it.

Two lobstermen sit on a boat. The sun hasn't risen yet. The world is very quiet. They're carefully looking away from each other. Paul checks the first lobster trap. No lobster.

They move the boat along. Next trap, no lobster.

And so on.

In the fifth trap, they catch a lobster, and Paul runs a finger down its spine to stun it, then puts it in the bucket. The lobster is too surprised to protest. Resetting the trap, Paul fumbles, stumbles, and Tom reaches out to steady him.

Their hands touch. It's a meet cute. That's not the right phrase. It's an excuse, and a moment later their hands are all over each other, they're kissing, they're gasping for breath in their rubber waders.

Reactions frequently trigger chain reactions. Restraint frequently does not last when put out of context.

But also, the sun isn't up yet. The end of the world is always safer when the sun isn't watching, when it's only the birds. The sun is a much less forgiving chronicler.

A bird caws overhead. The men break apart, flee to opposite sides of the boat (small, white, dingy, named for Tom's mother—Bernadette). Just in time for another boat to cruise in.

The lobstermen are not supposed to cross into each other's territories. It's the rule of the trade. But here's Julian and his band of cronies, and they're in the wrong territory.

Thank goodness Tom and Paul have something to distract them from themselves. The birds circle overhead. The sun is rising.

This is not a love story for the times when you refused to look at anything bigger than yourself, didn't want to contemplate it. When we say love story, we mean end of the world story.

Left to your own devices, you start punching brick walls. Playing bloody knuckles. It's a game with only yourself. It's not a very good game. Eventually you get blood everywhere.

Sharp and bright, and then you clean the knuckles with rubbing alcohol, and it stings and you cry out involuntarily. You don't mind any part of this, but when you look at your knuckles with an eye to the future, you think maybe it's time to go on to other pursuits. What these pursuits might be, you can't imagine.

What kind of apocalypse is the kind where there are no flames, no sudden death, no plagues? Where the sun rises and sets, where time passes and passes and keeps going on?

This is not an end of the world that I want to subscribe to, you think. No one hears.

The crows have already flown on to better perches. Your hands sting from the alcohol, from the scraping.

Here is the end of the end of world in Antarctica. We will get to the middle, later. Right now, we just know the end. We don't like the end, don't like the way things go, but it's even harder to talk about getting there. Here it is:

Lena runs out of the science station and into the snow. The snow is endless. It keeps falling.

The other scientists form a search party, go out holding a rope to keep them together, like small children trying not to get separated from their parents. They find her. She's fine. Hypothermia hasn't set in yet. It's fine. She knows snow, after all. She's not in an unfamiliar place.

Everything blurs in the snow.

The medical committee wants to send Lena home or at least to a place with more regular daylight, but the snow is too heavy.

They have to wait until it's safe for the planes or the boats to come. In the meantime, they keep careful watch. This is always the worry in Antarctica, that things like this might happen. Or always the worry with people, maybe.

Eventually, Lena leaves Antarctica, more or less whole. Eventually, separately, the assistant chef also leaves Antarctica, also whole. They do not leave together. They do not find each other again in the world outside of the snow. Neither really even tries. The world goes on. There are wars to fight.

Here is what all this feels like to the birds in their chests:

Dark and dark and dark and darker and that space inside the dark that is red and wet and waiting, an open mouth.

Bright and bright and bright, the aftereffects of looking at the sun too long. Scarring your retinas, so you can only see the afterimage.

Not enough space to stretch wings.

A constant, constant beating. A pulse.

Then it subsides for a while, so there's just the swish of wings beating against each other, against the darkness.

Some facts about Antarctica:

Once, many years ago, it was warm there and palm trees grew.

It's the place where all the time zones meet.

The top layer of ice is called a sheet.

Antarctica wants to tuck you in.

End of the world stories feel like getting really very tired. You don't want the world to end.

Let's repeat it:

You do not want the world to end.

The camera zooms in, focuses on hands again. They're aging more. The fingers are twisting around each other, nervous. Close-up on the veins in the wrists. They're pale. There's nothing here that hasn't been said before, but we stay on the hands longer and longer and longer, until it gets uncomfortable but still there are hands, and then you forget that they're hands. Start thinking of them as small mountains or weird animals or pieces of rubble. The fingers are still twisting around each other. There's nothing special about the gesture, but it does keep going.

At the archive of brightness, in the place with all the rocks, the crows are surveying their treasures. We have a lot of bright things, Cousin Jesse says thoughtfully, and the other crows agree.

What do we do with it? (He's plaintive.) No really, what do we do?

He keeps asking. His wings are flapping and he's getting more and more concerned.

What do we do with so many feelings?

They're shiny, and the crows would ordinarily be content to look at them, admiring them and making up stories about them, but Jesse's frantic. This used to be a safe place. It isn't that it's *not* a safe place now, but still. What do we *do* with all of them?

It isn't enough to just watch. There has to be action.

The crows huddle together. It's windy. The wind is blowing dust from the vulture's letters all over the rocks. It's getting in their eyes. There is so much of it all over.

Finally Crow Two raises a wing, tries to stand tall, says: I have an idea.

They're trying to make an imposing figure. Chest puffed out. Crows know all of each other's secrets. No one who's a bird has any secrets, anymore. They've been eradicated.

I have an idea, Crow Two repeats, more sure of themself now. The other crows settle down, listen.

So here's another story, Crow Two says. I heard it on the wind.

(Crows have a keen sense of irony, but like everyone else in this story, they choose to ignore it.)

A woman is spinning yarn from nettles. You know part of this story already. It's a very old story.

She is spinning yarn from nettles, and the scar tissue on her hands is building up, and she has long since stopped wincing. She's taken a vow of silence for seven years, and she's only half-way through.

(The crow looks like they have more to say about vows of silence, but then they shrug, do a casual wing flap.)

So this woman is silent, and she is spinning nettles, and her world is very quiet, with light shining in. There's light. It's cold light. It's light all the same.

Through the windows, the woman can see the seagulls fly across the sky. It isn't remarkable. It's commonplace.

(The crows do not love the seagulls, so this gets a round of applause.)

Crow Two is flustered, hops back and forth.

Crow One raises a wing, cocks her head.

Why is she spinning the nettles? she prompts.

Crow Two is relieved, ducks their head.

Let's pause here for a moment. We'll get there.

The two girls are leaving the graveyard, the one they went to when the end of the world was nearly a start. They're still crying. It's gross. They're both tired. The two girls try to leave the end of the world, but they can't find the highway. They're stuck in the middle of things, in the middle of mountains.

The sky is looking like rain again, just a little.

The two girls in the graveyard, they wanted everything to be all right. The two girls in the car, they just want to go home. They're existing at the same time, the same girls, always existing together. The girl who isn't driving is looking at the other girl, and she wants to say something about love, of all the things to say out loud, but the words get stuck in her throat.

They're still driving and they're still lost. If they were more lost, they'd drive off the edge of the world, but they're not quite there yet. Instead, they drive until they find the highway, then look for towns to stop in for lunch and don't find any. The end of the world stays with you, even after you're somewhere else.

The two girls are pointedly not talking about anything, the way you don't talk about things when you want to avoid just one subject so you avoid everything to be safe. The girl who is not driving looks at the girl who is, thinks she must be the most beautiful girl at the end of the world, says it.

It's a cliché, but not too bad. There are bigger clichés to worry about.

The other girl doesn't laugh. She looks like she might melt or cry, the way she always does with compliments. She squeezes the not-driving girl's hand, says thank you. Everything is serious when you've been at the end of the world. It's non-negotiable, this seriousness.

Nothing is funny about the end of the world, and everything is funny. Same thing, really. Comedy, tragedy. In the dark you can hardly tell the difference between the overarching themes.

It's getting dark both in the car and outside of it, and the girls are getting worried, but finally they see lights that they recognize. Not many, but a few. They get out and sit at a picnic table. They start out sitting on opposite sides of the table, but one of the girls does not like this, even if it lets her see the other one's face better, so she moves to where they can be touching.

Does it matter which girl?

One says or doesn't say, What will it be like after—

Snot gets in her throat. She successfully avoids crying and just looks down at the table, and together they find all the knots in the wood of the table, a small treasure hunt, and they stay quiet for a while. Bugs swarm in the air.

✳ ✳ ✳

After a pause, Crow Two wrote down their story, and now they're reading it from the stone.

For the crows, everything has to be permanent. They never write on paper. Maybe that's why the vulture's letters seem so dusty.

The woman is sitting and she's spinning nettles into yarn. Her hands are blistered, blistering. She's used to it. Seven years of silence, seven geese, seven shirts made of nettles.

How do you get a bird to wear a shirt?

Carefully.

The crows, who never wear clothes, scoff.

To be a bird or a flock of birds: these are choices.

To spin nettles into yarn or to never touch a spindle, these are some other choices.

Magic always requires a sacrifice. For the first three years, the woman doesn't mind the silence.

In her cold workroom, the only sounds are spinning and bird calls and her breath. Just now, it's winter, so she can see the puffs of air. Were this a different sort of project, the woman would be wearing gloves, but with magic pain is part of the equation. Nothing works without blood.

From the windows of the warehouse, she can see that the light is fading, pink and orange in the sky, and the geese fly down and come inside. During the time it takes for the sun to set completely, they are human again, and they are around her, and they are not even cold, not even really that changed.

The sun finally sets, and the laughter turns back into bird calls, and there are feathers everywhere all over again, and the geese duck out to go sleep in the grass by the river. The woman sighs, starts spinning again.

The way it began:

Just eight friends talking, but they talked too loud, made the wrong jokes, bantered in the wrong places. They went to a strange beachside town and they stumbled upon a candy shop and went inside.

The candy shop was suspicious, and ladies in ever more fluorescent shades of neon and brightly ironed aprons kept coming up to them and asking them if they wanted samples, and finally, to be polite, the friends took some. The woman who is spinning, who is not a bird, put hers back when the ladies were not looking. She didn't want their candy, didn't want to be in the store at all, had a bad feeling about the whole thing.

The others unwrapped the saltwater taffy, put it in their mouths, and almost didn't notice the ladies crowding eagerly closer and closer, and almost didn't notice suddenly all of the shop ladies' legs appearing, many more than you'd expect, and all in the wrong places, the feeling of wrongness sharply intensifying, but the woman who is not a bird noticed and grabbed her friends' hands which were not yet wings, pulled them out of the store and into her car, and then drove away and kept driving. They were all talking so fast that they barely noticed the shop ladies watching them from the windows of the store.

They escaped. For a while, the woman was a hero, and they all felt very brave, and they went to sleep in their separate apartments and thought they'd made a great escape.

The story could end like this, like safety and light, simple happiness. It doesn't, but it could.

The next morning, everyone except for the woman who is not a bird began growing feathers. They were still human in form, at least partially, so they spoke about it. They called each other on the telephones and congregated at one of the soon-to-be birds' apartments.

Luckily, they all lived close together, so no one had to drive. Some of the soon-to-be birds were already growing wingtips where their hands had been. None of them could wear shoes.

Everyone was changing, but the woman who was not remotely a bird stayed the same, and no one knew why. She couldn't figure out what was different.

They sat on the couches, looked at each other, talked about the circumstances and what to do and how this was probably a crazy shared hallucination, and the woman looked at her hands which had stayed hands this whole time and watched her friends slowly change.

The whole process took the length of a day. When the sun began to set, everyone was themselves again, and everyone was relieved, but once the sun was gone, everyone was a bird. Specifically, collectively: geese.

They looked at the woman and honked, and she could tell that they were distressed. You can always tell with the people you love, no matter what they change into.

So she lit candles, and sat and thought, and the birds huddled around. The woman tried to make her arms like wings, tried to be a mama bird to all the geese as they nestled in. She didn't have enough armspan, but it helped.

After hours of thinking, the woman began to do research. The reasons behind the transformation were unclear—in all of the old stories, people were turned into birds by jealous queens or evil witches, not tourist-trap shopkeepers. But whatever the why of it might be, the solution was evident. If the woman who was not a bird wanted to regain her friends, she would have to make some hard choices.

In the morning, the woman rose early and kissed all the geese on the space above their eyes, the space that on a person would be a forehead. She went off in search of nettles and eventually found some in a swamp just off the coast.

Supplies gathered, the woman who was not a bird went home and sat and looked at the geese for a while. She pulled up a chair and lit more candles for ambiance, knowing that sometimes rituals matter.

She fed the geese. The woman had looked up goose food on the internet in her night of frantic searching, and on her way home she'd bought them bread and grasses that a website said geese particularly liked. Also bird seed, just in case.

Then the woman began, one last time, to fill the empty space with words.

She started out by telling her friends how much she cared for them and how sorry she was that this thing had happened, even sorrier that it had happened without her, and then she moved onto her feelings about birds in general, which were primarily good.

The woman was afraid she would run out of topics, but she was committed, and the geese leaned in, listening carefully.

The sunset began. The woman spoke to all seven of her friends separately, earnestly, in the brief moment when they had human hands and tongues. They spoke back, sparingly. We are still us, was the main thing they wanted to say. We will love you no matter what you decide to do, was the second topic, but it was quieter and more implied.

She got a glass of water, made some notations on a calendar. Looked at her hands with unconcealed regret.

Then, all at once, the silence began. The spinning began, slow and fractured at first, producing messy, bloodstained yarn and then smoother, cleaner lengths. The geese kept watch in shifts, kept vigil. This had been decided. No one needed to talk about it.

They all slept in a heap on the woman's bed, a tangle of feathers and necks and one set of human limbs. It was a strange peace.

After the first uncertain weeks, the woman and the geese began to adjust to their new rules, their new way of being. You can adjust to anything if you try hard enough. The geese ventured out of the apartment to see the sky and heckle the ducks. The geese's possessions went into storage while their apartments were sublet, then the leases ended and they became other people's apartments. Enough money was made from selling a few big pieces of furniture to fund the geese's supply of bread for at least three years.

When the geese changed back to themselves at the start of sunset, it was not always an easy change like it had been at first. It was still instantaneous, but it's a lot easier to go from being one thing to another when you have more practice being the thing you're changing into.

At first, the woman who was not a bird's friends had been experts at being humans, and total novices about being birds.

But every day, they learned more about birdhood. About wings. About beaks. About swiveling necks.

They hadn't expected to like it, but they started to appreciate certain aspects of being geese more and more each day.

The woman hadn't expected to be so at peace with either the silence or the pain, but she had always felt as if she were at fault for something, and here was an opportunity to suffer for it. And the act of spinning was calming.

They went on like this for a while. Years of sun and geese honking and cool concrete. There was no sign of witches.

The crows, politely listening, have begun to shuffle their feet. They aren't looking the crow who's talking in the eye. Crows try very hard to be good listeners, but they're still birds, after all.

What we mean is that they're a bit flighty.

Crow Two notices the shuffling, pauses, says, Let's take a break. We're talking and I'm glad we're talking, but, you know. Let's take a break. Let's check in.

This has been a very long time to talk about geese, which, like seagulls, none of the crows really likes. They take a break, congregate on one tree, then another, and then another, flapping and cawing.

Crow One looks at Crow Two, nods her head. Good story so far, she caws.

Crow Two ducks their head, nibbles on their talon.

Crow One pats Crow Two on the shoulder with her wing.

Across the way, Cousin Jesse is pacing, murmuring *sacrifices require blood* as though it's the first time he's heard it. What a thought! As if the crows hadn't already had it carved in stone as a family motto.

The girl who's grown wings, who is a bird but not a bird, or maybe a bad bird, keeps jumping off rooftops. She's not trying to fly, exactly, but her wings pick up the wind every time.

She's wondering when and if this will end, if she can make it end. What do birds do?

(Lots of things. Flying, folding, fluttering, to name a few).

The birds watch her, but she doesn't see them watching, only sees the other buildings. Thinks, maybe if I get to the roof of the highest one.

When she is back in bed, surrounded by light, her wings cover her, catch the light.

The geese from the crow's story are currently in goose form. They haven't been humans yet today. They fly in a straight line to the duck pond, where they spend hours taunting the ducks. As humans, they liked ducks. Now?

Everything is changed.

Or everything is the same. The geese are very proud of their honking and waddling, and they manage to score a good-sized piece of bread.

In the end of the world that is a desert, a coffee shipment has just arrived and there is a great deal of rejoicing.

The filmmakers perk up for the first time in what seems like years, although it has probably not been years or even months. Days, anyway.

Time cannot be relied upon.

The filmmakers rejoice. They're smiling into their cups of coffee around the scorpion table. The townspeople rejoice. They have coffee and these filmmakers are not pining for it all over their nice town. The coffee shop owner is so busy brewing the coffee carefully, cup by cup, he almost doesn't notice that the house-builder still isn't there and that his sister is equally not there.

If he were to think about it, he'd wonder first if one of them had offed the other. They'd been bickering since they met. He would not think enough about it to see that fighting, too, can be a form of love.

For now, Darryl just thinks about coffee—not even thinks so much as concentrates on the careful, gentle pouring of hot water through filters into cups. It's a calming sensation. The water is beautiful as he pours it, and it's steaming even though it's very warm in the desert, warm and dry. Who even knows where this water is coming from? (The family of diviners finds it.) But it makes a perfect cup of coffee every time.

The scorpions, the live ones, aren't sure what to do. They've been scuttling around as usual, but something feels off, feels too quiet. They miss being filmed, having the camera's eye on their exoskeletons—a very different sort of gaze than the townspeople's. The people of scorpion town mostly look to them with an eye towards future home improvement. The film crew looks with fear and awe.

It's pretty clear what you would prefer if you were a scorpion.

The vulture in the corner has been dozing, as there hasn't been much happening, but then he wakes up with a start, sensing the change coming in the air: much like rain, although there's none of *that* here.

He picks up his feather pen.

The women in the scorpion house that the house-builder built for herself, they're kissing yet again, and it feels like they're not at the end of the world at all, and the house-builder wonders how she could ever have dreamed of a handsome, black-coffee-drinking carpenter. She knows deep down that she is still capable of that dream, but she keeps kissing the woman who does not drink coffee and who is not going to die, probably, at least not anytime soon. The woman who does not drink coffee's eyes are the most remarkable brown, the kind that has all kinds of different colors in it, the kind of brown that most people never comment on. It shakes the house-builder to her foundations, to her cornerstone.

Something in her stomach drops, which is another cliché, but you already know the desert and its lack of irony.

They keep kissing, and the house-builder's hands start tingling and losing feeling, and she wonders if this is what love is. A loss of feeling, or at least a restructuring. What if she can never feel her hands again? What if this is the sacrifice she has to offer for the end of the world to feel like a beginning?

The house-builder likes her hands, likes all the things she's built with them, but at this point in time she likes the weird tingling and the kissing more, and she likes the tiny points of light streaming through scorpion windows and scorpion blinds.

And the woman who is not dying, probably, and who does not like coffee? She's kissing with intention, with teeth and tongue, not just lips. She is unsure what she's feeling. Invisible strings, she'll think later. Not like there's a puppet master, just like there are threads between her and the house-builder, pulling them together. Like the strings you tie around your fingers for promises or reminders, but wrapped together in bigger, brighter ways.

Her fingers and hands, at present, are taking off the house-builder's cowboy hat, they're taking off her western shirt, they're removing all the trappings of the desert. The motion is careful and gentle, slowly but surely revealing the body beneath. Dust and sand swirl up with each article of clothing removed, and for a minute the woman worries that if she keeps unwrapping, eventually nothing will be left but dust. She will have taken off too many veils and found that the house-builder really is just the desert after all.

The woman who is not dying, probably, takes off the house-builder's denim pants, which is a challenge given that they're lying so close together that it's almost like sharing a skin, but she does it, slides them off, and the woman who is a house-builder shudders almost unnoticeably. The woman who is not dying checks in, says, Is this okay, but the woman who is a house-builder nods, pulls her tightly in, even more tightly, and they lie there together for a while, not saying anything at all, in unspeakable brightness.

And then the woman who is not dying, probably, continues with intent, gentle hands pulling off layers, and then suddenly the house-builder is naked and not made of dust at all, and the woman who is not dying is kissing her kneecaps and moving upwards, she's tracing flowers on the house builder's thighs with her tongue. It's silly but the house-builder is breathing very quickly and flutteringly, and so is the woman who is not dying.

The woman who is not dying does not know enough about the end of the world to be scared.

She does not know yet how close she is to the edge of things.

One of the filmmakers has woken up from the coffee, is carefully filming all this. The women don't notice.

The woman who is not dying starts to move in closer, but the house-builder, formerly paralyzed—not by fear so much as by care—moves suddenly. Then she is taking off the woman's dress, taking off everything, with no fear that anyone might turn to dust.

They are looking at each other with intent, and the woman who is not dying starts giggling, and the house-builder freezes, worried she's laughing at her, but the woman who is not dying shakes her head, says, I'm not laughing at you at all, you're gorgeous, I mean look at you. (This does not reassure the house-builder.) I'm laughing because how did we even get here?

And the house-builder's shoulders relax and she starts laughing too, and there they are in this house of scorpions. There they are.

The house-builder starts kissing the woman who is not dying, and they're still laughing in the kissing, and then suddenly neither of them is laughing at all, they are completely focused on the kissing, on their bodies, which are touching at all the junctures where they could be touching, and on the invisible threads pulling them together.

The vulture is politely averting his eyes but still trying to write everything down. This is all a part of the end of the world.

We're not gaining much with this discussion, so let's move on. They'll be there for a while. The things people say and don't say can go on for lifetimes, and, well, we don't have that kind of time, although we have some.

The end of the world is a puzzle, one of the crows says, watching.

The others nod.

It is something more and less than that.

A quick survey, while we're in an interlude. Is the moon watching any of this?

Yes. The moon is watching nearly everything.

Nearly?

Sometimes other things come up.

Does the moon have a stake in any of this?

The moon is very far away.

So it's a casual hobby?

Nothing with the moon is casual. You know that.

Yes.

She's watching right now.

It is very quiet here.

Yes.

The moon is not afraid of blood.

Well, no. Hadn't we better be getting back?

At the supermarket, the lobsters in their tanks are crawling around with a sense of urgency. Their antennae have been growing long, and they've been waiting and waiting, and while lobsters do not have the same sense of boredom that humans do, they still would prefer not to wait, would prefer to do anything else really.

The lobsters feel like they've been watching paint dry. They barely know what paint is, but it's that same soreness of process, lack of progress.

It isn't that they want to be eaten, it's that they want something to happen. Anything.

Tom and Paul enter the store, separately, and bump into each other in the candy aisle, literally. Tom trips and falls into Paul's arms and there they are for a second, holding each other in a grocery store, and then they quickly let go and look away.

I—Paul begins, but Tom shakes his head.

Tom changes aisles. They keep running into each other. They avoid eye contact, but they keep running into each other.

The lobsters in the tank perk their antennae up, can feel something in the air.

In front of the seafood display, Tom and Paul run into each other yet again, and Paul puts a hand on Tom's shoulder and says, Can I talk to you?

And Tom says, No.

But Paul's hand is still on his shoulder. He says, I really need to talk to you.

And Tom says, I don't think you do.

And Paul is looking at him now with careful intensity, and Tom likes it and doesn't like it, and he pushes Paul away, thinks he's being gentle, but Paul's balance is off,

thinks it's a tap, but Paul falls back against the lobster tank, which is supposed to be bulletproof but isn't; one side was replaced a few years back and the grocery store owner didn't think it'd be too much of a problem to replace it with just normal glass—

(after all, no one's shooting it, and normal glass is shinier— there was a a lack of shine problem with the old window, so the lobsters were not looking winsome enough to eat, and this was not ideal for anyone, although to be honest lobster sales have not been great in the interim either—)

—so anyway, the glass breaks as Paul hits it. There's blood on the floor as Paul lands, and the glass lands, and unfortunately his limbs land with the glass, on the glass. The blood is Paul's and it's all over. Humans have an impossible volume of blood.

The lobsters freeze, terrified and unsure, and then they realize they are free, and they wiggle their antennae in front of them and meander out of the puddle, away from Paul, and then scatter.

Lobsters in the baking aisle, lobsters in the frozen food aisle, a commotion of lobsters everywhere you turn, not a pod but a shield, or several shields, and people are screaming, and there's so much happening that almost no one notices Paul lying in a pile of blood and glass and briny saltwater. A single lobster stays to watch over him, feeling thankful.

Tom notices, of course, and he watches for a minute, tries to resist his urge to go to him, but he doesn't quite make it.

Paul is crying and it's mixing with the brine and blood, it's all metallic and salty. He's not hurt that badly, but the shock, and the pain.

Tom sits down next to him, says, I'm sorry, Paul. Says, Do you want me to take you to the hospital? Says, I guess we should talk about whatever you wanted to talk about.

But Paul's still crying like the world is ending, which it is; sobbing like someone who's heartbroken, which he is.

Tom is so embarrassed. He looks around to see if anyone is looking. A small crew of grocery store employees is coming their way.

He reaches out, touches Paul's hand, and grabs on.

That day with the other lobstermen out on the water, nothing happened. No altercation, no blood, not even threats or hostile looks.

Just seagulls circling in the sky, anxious lobsters in buckets.

Afterward, though, nothing about the space of time before sunrise felt safe. The crows noticed.

Two girls sitting on a porch swing, two girls in a graveyard, two girls lying in the backseat of a car with moonlight streaming in. One of them is reading poetry that she's copied out by hand, but she's lighting it up with her cell phone flashlight, and neither one can stop giggling. Technology is not always terrible.

Two girls sitting in the grass, looking at each other. One looks at the other's arms, and she can see faint scar tissue on them. It wouldn't be noticeable if she didn't know how to look, but once you know how to look, you can't stop looking. Like with everything else, the looking changes you.

She kisses the faint lines the next time she kisses the girl, and neither of them says anything about it.

There are many things you can know about another person without ever having to say anything. The girl is learning by increments, filling in gaps by the things that she looks at and immediately sees, and by the things that come later.

Two girls share a cigarette in a parking lot, look at the moon, look at each other looking at the moon. Two girls and this weird inventory of knowledge that neither one has asked for. Two girls under a blanket, two girls sharing a chair, two girls entwining and then shying away and then entwining again.

They're walking in the tall grass, and they're sharing another cigarette, a near-infinite supply of cigarettes, and everyone is around but just out of reach, and it doesn't matter anyway. One girl is wearing the other one's sweatshirt. The other one is shaking. Can't stop.

They're both crying. It doesn't matter anyway. The sun's setting, and it doesn't matter. One of them is leaving, and it doesn't matter. It's going to rain soon and this matters least of all.

It isn't noteworthy, but it's happening all the same. They're playing a game outside, and they're talking, and one girl starts crying uncontrollably and the other one clenches her fists, goes underwater, tries to breathe.

Two girls and they're outside, but it's raining. They're trying to read but it's raining. They're sharing an umbrella but it's still raining. The rain is covering the mountain, and the fog is rising, so that no one can get anywhere.

Two girls. They're tired.

They went to the end of the end of the world, and it hurt, but in some ways it was perfect. They went so far that it was hard to find their way back from the edge, and that was frightening. The night was cloudy, so nothing guided them, and it feels like that should have meant something, the making it back anyway, but here they are and everything is all wrong. Nothing is in perfect ninety-degree angles anymore. Everything is irregular and they can't even find the moon.

It's still the end of the world, of course, but they can't feel the urgency in it; everything just feels punctured. Like deflated balloons.

The end is not the end is not the end.

On the very last morning, no one's drinking coffee at all. They brush their teeth in the bathroom at the same time. They help each other get dressed. They cling.

Two girls and one is watching herself holding the other girl. She is trying to commit this to memory, etching it in her synapses. The girl who is leaving packs her bathroom things in her overnight toiletry bag.

The girl who is not leaving wonders when the girl who is leaving will notice the badly drawn anatomical heart on a scrap of paper, hidden in a pocket of the bag. If she will.

Outside, it's already raining again.

We'll be fine, one of the girls says, and they're both crying now, again, after all that. One leaves and the other one watches her leave, the way that her grandmother always watched their car pull out of the driveway after a visit, making sure the car was completely gone before she left the doorway. She waves the whole time the other girl's car is in sight, and then she goes inside.

It is quiet for a while, and everything is so entirely the same that it hurts. The world has chosen not to bear witness to this loss. It remains unchanged in the face of such a colossal absence.

She goes back to bed and it's still quiet. Not a deadening quiet, even, just the usual sort, unremarkable.

The end of the world waits until you aren't looking anymore to pounce. It's been waiting for this, but neither of them saw it until now.

No hands in sight aside from the usual two.

Bright lights, a lack of shadows.

When she wakes up later, the rain hasn't stopped, has picked up in fact.

CROW TWO: And we saw all of that?

CROW ONE: Yes. We did.

CROW TWO: Is this the end now? Are we finally at the end?

CROW ONE: For now. The world is always ending. You know that.

Crow Two nods. They're at the archive of brightness, look-ing at what's particularly shiny. Searching by color. This one is grey, but iridescent, like pigeon feathers or a particularly good silk.

Another crow's corpse has been found in the snow. No one's sure what to do. Crow funerals are a sea and sky of black. All noise. If they were humans, they'd be looking at their feet.

The snow has not stopped falling in Antarctica, but who expected it to?

Near the station, flags are blowing in the wind.

IV. The Beginning of the Middle

BACK TO THE BEGINNING OF THE MIDDLE:

The birds in the assistant chef and Lena's hearts are fluttering at the same pace. Some would call it monstrous. Certainly, they're flighty.

The assistant chef is coughing, choking on the feathers. Lena's been coming around to the kitchen every day this week, and every time it's a sudden jolt, a trip stair. After work, the assistant chef sits in a corner, looks into the corner and nowhere else, keeps looking.

Yes, of course, the looking changes you. We all already know this. You look, and then you can't look away or you can, but either way you've been forever marked. It is exhausting, this world, even as it ends. Especially as it ends.

The assistant chef, if asked why she came to Antarctica, would struggle to find an answer. There were reasons. The vast empty whiteness. The penguins (she'd always liked penguins). The freedom of going to a place where she didn't know anyone, where the people would always be coming and going in constant rotation.

Really, what it had come down to was the fact that there was an open job, and she had a feeling, what you might call a hunch, and then she applied, and now here she is. Looking into corners. Looking at hands. Relentlessly, endlessly looking.

In the kitchen, she plans elaborate menus for the scientists, pulls off themed dinners based on different cuisines from around the world, television shows, even colors. In the laundry room, the lab coats are always sparkling. The assistant chef's job is care.

In the kitchen, she tries to focus as Lena says something about explorers. She holds very still, a prey animal in a forest. They look at each other for a minute. A sudden jolt of eye contact, of knowing. The birds in their chests stay very still.

There was a crow, and then there was another crow, and then there are three, four, until they are innumerable. An endless supply of birds, endless and uncountable, but they keep losing crows at an unsustainable rate. Even if they're innumerable, you can still subtract, can still feel absence.

The crow funerals are quiet now; they are lines, not shapes. The birds are wondering how to make sense of any of this, and whether, perhaps, they should just stop, let the archive erode, stop watching, look instead at the corners.

There is nothing in the corners, that's the point; but if there's nothing, it can't hurt them, which is also the point. No points in a line. Just feathers, shuffling. Birds don't cry. Can't.

No tear ducts, maybe.

In the sky they don't look like birds so much as a battalion, an army, a beginning. You can't pick out a single crow in the sky, you can only see that there's a murder. You can only see the sum total of them, the vastness of all together at once.

This is how birds get power.

(Do birds want power?)

Birds want to know things. They want it very badly, the knowing.

Feathers scatter everywhere, feathers drift apart. They're making a black dust along the snow.

To be a bird isn't a choice, but to be several birds at once is. To look or look away, or look nowhere at all, this is another choice. And it's a hard one, in truth, it always changes the looker, but the crows—

(none of them ever pecks out their own eyes, and none of them pecks out the eyes of their crows-in-arms; they never look away)

—but maybe—

(they never look away, except to be polite, and even then they are looking, because birds, you know, they can see different things out of each of their eyes; they aren't like humans)

—birds are nothing like humans at all.

You don't know how many crows there are, but you can see them multiplying, a black, feathery mass. All different, all the same, landing in the melting snow.

Night comes to Antarctica, but how would anyone know it? It's been dark for months now.

Lena is dreaming about snow. It's covering her. It's like static, but also yarn and thread, so it's more the idea of snow than the literal substance. It's tucking her in like a blanket. She's sleeping in the lab coat now. She wonders if she made a mistake coming to this place. Everything is quiet, but it's the sort of quiet that's breathing. You can't count on this sort of quiet. It might jump out at you in the dark.

The assistant chef dreams about birds. They are all watching her, not with malice, just watching, all solemn bird pupils and arching beaks. No calls. No flying.

The birds are in a line, and they are very still, and they are waiting.

The assistant chef is not sure what they're waiting for, but she wakes up suddenly and keeps her eyes shut, stays there in uneasy, unseeing awakeness until she falls back asleep. After that it's hands again, just like all the other nights.

Hands: they're gnarled and aging, they're getting tired, but they're wringing each other, wringing each other's necks. She isn't sure if she's dreaming or just thinking, but in the dark they are mostly the same thing. In the darkness, the hands become Lena's, Lena's hands kneading bread. The bird in the assistant chef's chest flaps its wings so fast that she feels choked up.

In the quiet darkness, everyone is thinking very loud and fast. The birds are making nests.

Crow Two clears their throat nervously, waiting to begin. Well—they start to say, but the words are swallowed up.

We're back at the archive of brightness. There are more words on the stone. They glint. The other crows aren't listening; they're nudging each other, cawing about the weather.

Crow Two claps their wings—no response.

Crow Two begins to caw loudly, and the other crows look up, surprised.

Back to storytime, Crow Two says meekly, and the other crows nod. Settle in with resignation to listen to the story about geese.

By the fifth year, all the yarn was spun and the woman had started knitting shirts for the geese. Sweaters, really. Cardigans, to account for wingspans—it'd be hard to get anything on over their heads.

By the fifth year, the geese who had once been people were a lot more goose than person. The sunset change was becoming more brutal, more wrenching. None of them ever knew what to do with their hands or what to say in their brief moments of human form. It made the woman tired, watching this, and she wondered: is the reprieve a part of the curse? Would they be better off just staying as geese?

But the woman who'd made a vow of silence couldn't ask her friend-geese, and wouldn't have, even if she could. She missed her friends. She missed having them around as humans for always and not simply for a brief time each night.

The silence wasn't too much of a problem, and the pain wasn't too much of a problem, and the knitting became almost enjoyable as time went on. In the middle of the fifth year, the woman met someone. A person. The kind of person who was always a person and not only sometimes.

The woman fell in love instantly, or at least fell into something instantly. There was a moment of nothingness, and then a trick stair moment, a brightness in the veins moment. This was unexpected. She wondered if it was a test, if the universe was trying to see if she really deserved to get her friends back. She looked at the sky as if to ask, but the sky looked away first and refused to answer.

She resolved not to engage with this test.

The person in question, the one who was presumably always a person, had begun working in the upholstery shop nearby. She always saw them on her walk to work, a walk where they always waved and asked her questions she couldn't answer, looking at her with their smile and all of their teeth. The geese saw them as well and watched speculatively, wondering what this would mean. Considering the possibilities, they scared some ducks thoughtfully, flapping their wings and honking.

The woman shivered in her workshop, lit only by a cold light, her hands developing scars on scars on scars. Three goose cardigans were done. All the nettles were spun. Things were soon to be coming to a close.

In the end of the world in the desert, everyone was fully awake. The brief quiet spell had been nice, had been a period of hiding, a time of building, but then the coffee came back. The filmmakers were twitching. The townspeople were eagerly awaiting new scorpion structures.

Secrets only last so long in small towns.

Everything had been safe in the scorpion house, with the coffeeless town fast asleep, and the women had got along swimmingly. Now they had to exist within a larger sphere. Now things were getting tense and overdrawn; life couldn't just be kisses on foreheads and childhood stories. The easiest way to destroy something is to put it up against the whole world.

What a nightmare, thought the woman who was no longer at serious risk of dying, sitting in her own house. What a terror, thought the house-builder, now back in her cowboy boots, cowboy hat, and denim.

The vulture kept flying back and forth between them, wings abuzz.

You and my sister seem to be getting on like a house on fire, says Darryl the coffee shop owner, and the house-builder nods politely, says, I hope we're getting to be good friends.

Darryl doesn't know yet about anything that's happened, only that the house-builder and his sister were fighting, were like cats circling, and now they're getting not-coffee together, walking along the cliffs. Darryl isn't stupid. He's just glad his sister's made a friend.

The house-builder is drinking coffee, thinking about the meaning of the phrase *house on fire*, how it's meant to be a good thing. But a house on fire, that's a thing that's burning. Houses on fire self-immolate. What kind of praise is that?

The vulture in his corner, he's frantically writing and hoping that his words get to the crows fast enough, hoping that he says the right things at the right times.

He's wondering how to change this end of the world. When it was quiet and blue, and lit only by stars, it was going so well, but now there's desert heat and dust and film lighting, and it's a different dust, and a different kind of ending. He can feel it in his lungs.

The filmmakers, shooting quietly from a distance, are starting to look like birds, all aflutter. They also know that they're at a critical juncture. The woman who does not drink coffee, she's sitting in her house fiddling with the pillow tassels, and the filmmakers are filming her hands over and over again, and from the dark corners the scorpions are watching, wondering, waiting. The end of the world in the desert feels as if it's happening very fast, yet there's nothing much to see. It seems like there should be lambs or flash floods or vast external signs, but the end simply unfolds and keeps unfolding. This end of the world is, it would seem, endless.

The wind blows, the sand shifts. Everything becomes slightly different.

No one can go anywhere while the sand is blowing. The filmmakers take shelter. The vulture sighs and puts down his letter, knows it won't be mailed anywhere tonight.

Want to know what happens next? says the storytelling crow, and the other crows re-focus on this shining brightness instead of all the other shining brightnesses, brighter than aluminum foil or diamonds or lobster pots.

The woman who is knitting is quietly in love.

She wonders, while she's knitting, how anyone could love someone who's a cipher, how anyone could love someone with this many scars, but she can't say anything. The geese would like to help, but they never have enough time as humans. It takes too long to remember how to live in their skins, how to form words with tongues or flex fingers. The person who works at the upholstery shop, they notice a gaggle of birds always nearby, but they don't think too much of it. Where they are from, there are always birds.

The geese have noticed the person working at the upholstery place, but for the birds, they are not a jolt of electricity. Maybe they would be if they started really looking, but there's an awful lot of bread in the pond down the street, and far too many seagulls to fight, to worry about this.

The woman finishes the last sweater, feels this strange sense of emptiness. There's some time left where she has to stay silent, but the task is otherwise done. She wants to give the sweaters to the geese now to see if it will break the spell, but has it really been enough time? Has she really done enough? She wonders about the nature of goodness, the feeling of deserving.

The geese, privately, think they'll look ridiculous in sweaters. How could anyone put a bird in a sweater if not for the express purpose of freeing them from what binds?

Although, it has been cold this winter, and they never fly south because they don't want to leave her, and it would be difficult to explain in the changing, and if they refuse it could be a colossal disappointment, so—fine, the geese will wear the sweaters. The woman helps each of her friends into one, carefully, wing by wing. She buttons the buttons, one by one. They all wait, patiently, nervously, filled with expectant silence.

No word from anyone, nothing changing; light through the windows. Other birds, untethered by nettle sweaters, flying above. The geese know that the other geese they've been palling around with are going to give them shit about the sweaters.

(At this, the crows begin to laugh, imagining the geese's embarrassment, and for a few minutes it's too loud, the laughter, for the storyteller to continue.)

The light begins to fade. The birds are changing into humans, but humans wearing too-small, scratchy sweaters, struggling to remember how joints work, why they can't swivel their heads. They finally remember, compose themselves, stay very quiet and wait—

—and then the light is gone entirely. It's night, so the only light is from the stars, and you can barely even see the stars on account of the city's pollution, and yet—

the flock is still human. They still have hands, still have noses, don't have wings. They're a bit disappointed and a bit mistrusting, but it's also all kinds of exciting.

The woman doesn't even see it—she's already fallen asleep, exhausted.

And the bird-people, they fall asleep on the floor around her, all still wearing their sweaters, afraid that if they take them off, something terrible will happen. Afraid they'll unravel, be undone.

There is much to fear, even when you've come out the other side of something. Seven years feels like an eternity, and it isn't even done yet. Everyone's eyes shut—their human eyes—and they hope for the same eyes to open in the morning.

The crows are reading the vulture's last missive and frowning, shaking their heads. There is not so much that glimmers in this one, just a lot of worry. It oozes off the page, it's everywhere, a thick sludge. The crows cough and try to rid themselves of the worry, try to replace it with other, better things like tin spoons or cinnamon toast, but it clings. It's like an oil spill. The crows have never been caught in an oil spill, but they've heard about them from friends and this feels similar; it's dragging them down.

Coughing, coughing, the sound of many crows coughing.

Crow One looks at Crow Two, says, That was a good story, says, I'm glad you shared it, and Crow Two blushes as much as a crow can blush but also says, It's not over yet.

Crow One nods solemnly, says Yes, I've seen you working on the stone tablets.

Crow Two is surprised and flattered that she's noticed, looks down, flaps their wings shyly.

CROW TWO: Yes. They still have to sacrifice more. It can't
     be that easy.
CROW ONE: Things rarely are.

They stand in silence, are joined by several more crows. They fly from tree to tree and the moon is shining, and people stop to watch them, try to take video on their phones, but in the darkness the crows just look like more darkness, at least to a cell phone camera. Black radio static.

The crows do cartwheels in the air. Show-offs. It's just that they're happy, and the feeling is unfamiliar. It's such a relief.

Things are speeding up. It must be the moon.

The girl with the wings, she's found the tallest building she's ever seen, and she's charmed a custodian to get rooftop access. She's flapping her wings at the very top. It's quiet up here apart from the constant rushing of wind.

Her wings are ready. This is what they've been waiting for. The girl, she's not so sure. Here everything is, all coming down at once, all coming to a head.

It's so quiet and dark, dark. The lights from the buildings obliterate the stars. The girl looks around but doesn't see any birds. If they're around, they're being quiet too.

She takes a deep breath, lets her wings go free, and jumps, and for a while it is just like falling. She's afraid she's moving too fast, but the wings flap of their own accord. The wings want to save themselves. Then she's caught on a breeze and she's flying, flying, flying, and the birds all breathe a sigh of relief. They had been imagining Icarus.

She looks at the light coming from the buildings below—it's strange to see them from above. She keeps going but doesn't know where she's going. The birds lose track of her and look away, and then below her everything is black.

The girl wonders if she's taken a wrong turn, if there has been a power outage or sudden terrorist attack, and then she realizes that it's simply the water. By the time she realizes, it's too late. Her wings aren't strong enough, and she's falling again, faster and faster.

She lands in the water. The girl can do many things, but none of them involve swimming. She falls and falls, and suddenly she can't breathe, and then less suddenly she's thinking of Icarus too, in the aftermath, and then she is not thinking about him anymore.

Underwater, everything is loud, and she thinks, maybe I'm not meant to be a bird. The wings are weighing her down. The pressure is too much and she can't breathe and it all goes sun-spotty. Bright imprints on her retinas.

The birds didn't see her fall, but they have a feeling that something has gone awry. They circle the sky, looking for the girl, but she's nowhere to be found. Everything is so still. The birds shiver, then return to their nests for the night. There's nothing to be done. No stars in the sky tonight.

Later, Crow One says that there are always stars in the sky, and another crow nods but looks down and says, Maybe it would have been better for there not to have been.

Two girls together at the end of the world, but no one can see them except as a single unit. Two girls, but one leaves and the other one is a ghost. Everyone at the end of the world has buried their sense of irony beneath the poison of the goldenrod. One half of a person is gone and the other one's just a haunting, a shadow of a shadow; no one can see her. Standing in the dark under the moon; no one can see her. Ghosts buried beneath the trees, buried in the graveyard; there has been a subtraction and the man who runs the gas station can't even remember one girl on her own. Ghost on the porch swing; the weight's off with one person missing. The end of the world feels different when alone. The ghost looks at her hands and they're vanishing. They're disengaging, breaking apart at the wrists.

Shadows show where the light has gone. If there are two shadows, there are two sources of light.

We are sleeping and we are dreaming and we are waking up and we are sleeping and we are dreaming and we are waking up and we are sleeping and we are dreaming and we are waking up and we are sleeping and we are dreaming and we are waking up and we are dreaming and we are dreaming and we are dreaming—

This is the interlude before the story keeps going, Crow Two says, and not a joke or a mistake; the other crows believe it. You can look at them and see them believing. They're thinking about the things they ought to file better, ways to make the archive work, but they believe Crow Two. They believe the story.

Crows will do nearly anything for something with a lovely shine. More so, they will do nearly anything for a chance to make the world in front of them look like it aligns.

It is hard work to make meaning out of things that might be meaningless, but the crows are trying anyway. They remind themselves of their task when it is dark, and they are afraid, and the shadows are encroaching. Sometimes, often, they believe that their work is nearly at a close, their certainty a compass to follow, pointing due north.

We're back, says Crow Two, firmly.

We are waking up waking up waking up—

The bird-people all wake up and they're still humans and they're still wearing impossibly scratchy sweaters. And then, with a start, the woman who is not a bird wakes up and she looks at them, and she thinks it's sunset at first. You can see her processing. Suddenly, she realizes.

The woman who is not a bird puts a scarred hand to her mouth, tries not to let out any sort of sound.

There is a catch, she is thinking. It is unclear what the catch is, but it has not been quite seven years and there must be a catch.

The catch comes when the human from the upholstery store walks into the workshop, just opens the door and comes in, and they ask her if she'd like to go to dinner. They've clearly worked up to it for some time. She nods but doesn't say anything, won't say anything, and her friends also stay silent. Everyone is terrified that one wrong word will break the spell, and the human from the upholstery store looks around, looks confused, leaves. I'll be back, they call, on their way out.

It's a trap, the friends do not say, and the woman does not say, I know, but maybe—

They are all thinking these things, and they all know.

The bird-people will not take off their sweaters. They're too concerned about the prospect of becoming birds again, not that they wouldn't enjoy it but that they'd enjoy it too much. They miss flying. They have terrible dreams.

The woman who is not a bird has terrible dreams too, but hers are about her friends all leaving again, about accidentally speaking and changing everything for the worse. She wakes up shaking every night. They play silent card games in the workshop, and the light streaming in grows a little less cold, but every night feels a little like a wake, like something not to be trusted.

The person who works at the upholstery shop keeps coming by and then finally doesn't, and the woman is sad but relieved at the same time. After all, it is not like she is alone now.

The last year comes to an end. They sleep tangled, a pile of limbs. On the first morning of the eighth year, the woman doesn't say anything. No one says anything at all, at first.

Little by little, the words begin. The sweaters come off. Where there were big holes in the sweaters (the ones that were the woman's first attempts), the bird-people still have feathers—just a few, not enough for anyone to think much about. If the woman regrets the damage to her hands, and if the others regret their loss of flight, no one says anything about that.

The crows are silent. They're thinking this end of the world is a vast plain. They're thinking, Everything is very different than we thought it would be when we were young.

It's true. It's high noon, but the sky is grey.

Everything is changed. Everything is much the same.

The crows feel an overwhelming grief, which they've been feeling all along, but now more so. They try to imagine losing their flight, losing their ability to caw. It feels unthinkable, but so do the murders, the murders of members of the murder of crows. They wonder if anyone is trying to keep a record of their story, to make sense of it. Wings fidget in the grey.

Everyone looks at their toes.

Long silence.

Longer.

It's finally broken by a missive from the vulture in the desert at the end of the world.

Sand and dust get everywhere. The crows cough. No one is pleased. No one is making eye contact with either of their eyes. The vulture has no idea that he makes things such a mess. He's used to the sand.

The scorpions gather. They're worried—they're barely a part of this story, except as furniture, as set dressing; we mostly don't even notice the ones that are alive, but they're a hovering mass around the edges, a crunching set of family members. They're watching the filmmakers with suspicion.

It isn't that they keep any archives of their own, but they do want to make something out of something else. The scorpions know that everything is bought with a sacrifice. After all, they have become houses, they have become espresso machines, they have become metaphors for women falling in love or despair, but they are willing to risk it to become something that people find beautiful. It isn't a choice, really; they've been scooped up by fate and the house-builders, and yet they're willing anyway.

The scorpions would like the filmmakers to leave. They would like some things to stay private.

Not everything is meant to be a performance.

The vulture is worried for other reasons. He hasn't heard from the crows in a while, even though he's been writing earnestly, trying to get it all down. Frequently he can write only pictograms, but he was hoping the crows would give him a solution. It's the end of the world, and he's terrified.

If they get this wrong—

A desert is a desert is a desert. The sand covers everything, or the rocks cover everything, or in certain deserts everything is just naked and barren, but here there is sand and it has not covered everything yet: Look at these houses. Look at these people and the ways in which they fit together and the ways in which they do not.

The dust is getting thick in the vulture's throat. The filmmakers are filming, but it's getting a bit cluttered for their cinematic shots, even when the best boy captures a group of scorpions looking furtive. The vulture clasps a feather pen. They film Darryl with his espresso machine. The house-builder and how she kisses the forehead of the woman who does not drink coffee when she is already asleep, and how the woman who does not drink coffee smiles faintly, even while dreaming.

The filmmakers know that she is not yet asleep, at least half the time, when this happens, but they do not say so. It would be rude, unthinkable. And yet, they are not normally the sort of people who are known for tact. They're known for other things: panoramic shots, clear sound recordings.

The vulture reminds himself of these unexpected displays of

tact sometimes, when he gets especially worried, but really, he would like them to leave anyway.

He would like to steal their tapes and transfer their contents to a more stable format, something less likely to break down in the sun. Impermanent things must still be archived. This is a basic truth. Nothing is permanent on its own, not if enough time goes by.

The vulture wishes the filmmakers hadn't noticed the women, simply because their noticing means that other people can notice. You can't see what isn't there, but they are there, they're sitting on a cliff at sundown and it's a Western, it should have a shootout, but they're just talking. They're making meaningful eye contact, but the house-builder's hat is blocking our view of her eyes, casting them in shade.

They're green, her eyes. Nothing else is green in the desert. The woman who does not drink coffee and is probably not dying, she looks at them for a long time. She can't see them right now, not really, but she knows, so she fills in the blanks and goes from there.

Love is like this sometimes, full of details that you aren't quite making up but that you only know from a long time ago. Love is seeing the past every time, even if the present is different. Even if the present isn't quite as good, you see the moment when you saw her eyes, and they were like a cornfield in Indiana. And you see them again, her eyes, but framed in that light. Everything else is storytelling.

They keep making eye contact and no one says anything, and from one corner the scorpions are watching and hissing a bit, tails twisting in the darkness, and from another corner, the filmmakers are watching and tapping their equipment, leaning in with microphones to make sure they catch every word, and the vulture is in a third corner, writing it all down, and how many corners are there at this cliff in the desert at the end of the world?

The women don't know that there's even one corner. They think it's an infinite plane. To be fair, they also don't know it's the ending of anything.

Darryl comes walking through the desert toward the cliff, and he's not coming from a corner at all. He's walking across the plain plain, but the sand covers up his footsteps and the wind covers up the sound of him walking. He's not trying to be subtle, but neither woman is looking for him and they don't see him coming. They don't notice anything but their own mythology.

You can tell that by the way the house-builder is playing with her hands. By the way she's playing with them, touching them and wishing that she were touching the woman who does not drink coffee.

You can tell by the way the woman who does not drink coffee is staring. It's embarrassing, or it would be if we were somewhere where people had heard of cynicism, but that's mostly been left out east with the non-scorpion building materials. She's staring with the kind of intensity that painters wish they could capture. The kind that memorizes tiny details.

The painter would be blushing. The sun's in the house-builder's eyes, or at least its shade. She probably isn't staring, or if she is, we can't capture it on film.

Where is the light? the filmmakers are asking.

It's right here, and here, and here.

It's everywhere.

In a moment the women on the cliff will kiss again, and from all sides the scorpions and the filmmakers and the vulture and the woman who does not like coffee's brother will lean in, and the moment will be broken, and everyone will be changed for it. Maybe not the kind of change that you mark on your calendar, maybe not the kind that you can point to at the time, but change all the same.

In colliding with others, things become definite, things that have hitherto only existed in an in-between space. No one and nothing can hide from this law.

But for now, the light is everywhere. The filmmakers are thinking about the stories they will tell their families, the ones about birds and about waking up every morning feeling safe and warm and blessedly wingless.

The vulture is thinking of the letter he will send to the crows once everything changes. He's wondering how it will change because that is unpredictable, that is a precipice he can't see beyond. Darryl is thinking of how nice it is that his friend and his sister have gotten so close, but he can barely see them—the sun's in his eyes, and he doesn't have a cowboy hat. The house-builder and the woman who is probably not going to die, at least not any time soon, they are thinking, separately, of each other. They are thinking about the places where they are not. They are glad not to be in these places.

The scorpions are thinking about being scorpions, about what it means to be a scorpion, about what it means to be. They're enjoying the last rays of sunshine hitting their exoskeletons. They are tired, and they want to go to sleep, but they know that something is coming.

Change is coming. Isn't it? But we've already arrived at the end of the world. We are already farther than we ever thought we'd be. Close your eyes.

You wanted to write a better story, so you thought of birds. You were always talking about birds, back then. At least, you were always talking about seagulls, and about wings—talking, talking, talking.

In her absence, you remember that she didn't like birds and never looked at the sky with any intensity of feeling, perhaps was not interested in the sky at all, but that doesn't change anything. Even now, the world is made up of her negative space, the places where she isn't, all the places totally vacant of birds and of her.

We could go on like this forever. It wouldn't be terrible. It would just be us dissolving until anyone would be hard-pressed to find one solid piece.

Here is a piece of metaphor or memoir that you have barely considered yet: Consider the word consider, which means to look at the stars. Consider her reading a book on the floor of your room, awkward long legs all askew, a dim light on. Consider yourself, walking in and looking at her and deciding—one clear unbroken moment—and, later, your hands touching in the moonlight in a very quiet field on a cold and quiet night. In this way, things aren't unchanged exactly, they're just naked. They're laid bare.

Every time you looked at her, you saw the universe, but that's the story everyone tells and it isn't even a good one. You looked at her once, twice, and more, and after all of the looking, you couldn't stop considering, couldn't stop looking at the stars. It took years to look at the moon again.

Love does not make anyone a better writer. It does make them tired.

There is a shark in the ocean that will try to swallow everything it comes across, everything in its path, no matter if it's garbage or toxins or you. Love is like this, a constantly open maw where all of the good gets mixed in with plastic soda tabs and the like, and you ignore it for as long as you can, but you can't escape it. Either the love or the garbage—they're all mixed up together. Eventually, the sharks will die from the toxins.

But—you say—sharks do not archive anything, and that's true, whereas the crows certainly do: they've worked very hard to craft things out of the limestone. Their beaks have been sharpened. Those scarecrows won't know what hit them next time they swoop out of the sky: this is what the crows have been thinking, and they are very smug. They've been waiting for this sharpness for ages.

The archives, they keep following you. You shut your eyes but you know they're following. You imagine being a bird. Going to the top of anything worth getting to the top of, to get a better vantage point. Anywhere you are, though, the light is still there.

✳ ✳ ✳

Let's rewrite the story of the girl with wings. We're excavators, we're filmmakers, rewinding the tape. She's falling into the water, but now she's falling out of it, she's rising, and her wings are working in ways we never dreamed of, in ways wings have never worked before.

Zooming in, we can see the wires. The harness. The stunt double. We're splicing in reels of birds, we're splicing out the part where the wires are too bright against the sky, we're re-adding the plot and intrigue, we're taking away the other parts, the ones where we get too afraid. The ones where we start to believe that she's really growing wings, really unraveling in the sunlight.

She's flying and we don't even mind that it's a stunt. We can't be upset that she isn't really a bird when we're just glad that she's out of the water, out of harm's way. But it's not a very good Icarus myth if she's neither too close to the sun nor the water.

Let's bury this thought at the bottom of the sea, right along with the feathers that look like they've been ripped from skin, the bloodied ones. The water is washing the blood away. It's drawing the sharks but they can't figure out where it's coming from. It's buried and put to rest. Maybe later someone will find it and call it Atlantis, or maybe someone will find it and call it a home.

The girl is flying. You can see the safety wires, but it's good, because it means that she's safe, far from harm. It is hard to believe that we were ever worried. Hard to believe that the stars went out of the sky and the birds looked away, and everything faded to black. Hard to believe how quiet everyone was that night when we could see through the smoke and mirrors. When we could see the mechanics, the motors in the wings, the god in the machine.

Later the filmmakers will go home and tell their families about flight, will keep watching the footage of the birds and inspecting each other's shoulder blades daily, hoping for a change, wishing for it even, in their new, rewritten world.

And the girl?

This isn't her story anymore. She's written herself out of the story. She's underwater, struggling to rip out her wings, but it's difficult because they aren't a trick wire or a harness. She's pulling out feathers and feathers are pulling out skin and muscle and bone. Bird bones, but they're hers, so—just bones. She's not sure what she is. Maybe a bird. Maybe something else. Not better than a bird (what could be better than a bird?)—just different, maybe.

This girl, she can't breathe with all this pressure. She can't break the surface with her wings caught.

The filmmakers' catechism:

We will wake up in the morning, every morning, and it will be a new day. We will always see the sky. We will never question the stars. We can't look too deep inside the ocean, and neither can the birds. They're not even water birds.

We will make every morning new, make them all in our own image. We will only make promises we can keep. We will show you the wires.

We will know that a bird is a bird is a bird, and the birds, they will always keep you safe. They will always make sense of what there is to make sense of, and even what is senseless.

This we promise you. This we and the birds promise you. We hold out our pinkies, they hold out their wings. Our promises don't hurt us. That's how true they are.

The girl with wings, she'll always be on the cusp of something wonderful, and we will never have to think of danger except to be relieved about what's not happening. This we can promise you.

The girl promises other things, underwater, but you can't hear them. The ocean is very loud. It is shouting.

When the filmmakers find themselves in the quiet, lonely depths of their thoughts, they are hoping that none of them, the filmmakers nor their families, ever wakes up with a mass of feathers. They are hoping no one ever looks too deeply into the water. They are hoping no one climbs to the tops of the highest buildings.

Tom and Paul are holding hands. They aren't on the lobster boat, aren't wearing their rubber waders, aren't even completely alone.

What do the circumstances matter?

Paul is blissfully happy.

Soon, other emotions will find him again, but we'll leave before they do. The lobsters, the ones that escaped in the glass tank accident, they've gone out to sea. They're not going to be fooled by salted herring again. They're going to stay squarely on wet sand, feet buried deep. They're going to molt in peace.

The day is ending. Let's finish with a soothing story.

Tom and Paul are looking into each other's eyes and noticing all the colors in them, the way that they aren't ever simply one thing. The sun is fully up. This is not happening under the light of the moon.

This end of the world ends with this moment. Don't blink.

Back in Antarctica, it is still snowing, and the snow is erasing all trace of anything. There's no point in talking about the ending here: we already know. The ending is that it keeps on snowing.

We are not saying this to make the story sad, but it's true: nothing good is going to appear. Nothing can grow in Antarctica. That's been true from the beginning. Or if good does come, that good will be fractured, complicated—certainly a mixed bag. Lena will run out in the snow, will be saved, will leave eventually. The assistant chef will leave too, but differently, perhaps with less fanfare. The snow will go on falling. It will not always fall in the same way, but it will always fall. The things underneath it won't go away, but they might not stay where you left them. This is not a metaphor, just endless white.

Here is another moment in Antarctica, before all of this business with Lena and the chef. Everyone has gone outside together to look at memories projected on the snow. They're huddled together there, shivering, white parkas and white lab coats and white chef coats all blurring against the snow.

The projector begins to roll, and the scientists and staff hush each other.

It begins the way it always begins. Babies, learning to walk. Corgis running through leaves. A punk rock concert where everyone is looking at their shoes. Cars and shadows; cars and city lights (another thing Antarctica lacks). A couple slow danc-ing at a bar. The projections flicker and flicker against the snow, and the projector whirs, and everyone holds their breath to see if it's stopping, if the show is done, if it's time to go back inside and focus on the present.

The projector clicks on again. There's an outtake where everyone breathes through their scarves and muffs, and you can see the breath against the darkness of the sky even though it blends in with the snow that is constantly falling. If they stay outside for long enough, their hats and coats will be covered with big fluffy flakes.

Every snowflake is different, but at the same time they're all frozen, all falling, all getting caught on everyone's glasses or eyelashes or safety goggles.

For some people this is very romantic, and these are the sorts of people who choose to go to Antarctica, who think that the winter is something wonderful to keep ahold of.

The projections start again. Something new: it's Lena and the assistant chef in the kitchen. The assistant chef has flour on her nose. They're laughing, laughing and talking. Lena is help-ing to knead bread. The assistant chef is organizing pots on the industrial stove. Other people are there, but as usual, they're all background noise.

The thing about the projections is this: they are shown in third person, from the point of view of someone watching overhead, like the way memories sometimes work in your mind as well. You're both in and out of the frame at the same time, as if you're both the cameraman and the star actor. This can get confusing, but it helps everyone watching to fill in the blanks.

The other thing about the projections is that, for the most part, they are not of Antarctica. They are of life's warmest moments. They show the things people think of in the dark when they are missing home or each other or something else big in the universe. That is, the things that people miss in Antarctica are things far away from Antarctica, far away from ice or snow. Mostly, summer.

The projector moves on from the laughing in the kitchen, onwards to other big moments that shine in the darkness. Most of the people in the crowd don't even think twice about it. Lena and the assistant chef though, they're both frozen in the crowd. The assistant chef has been counting hopes like rosary beads as she embroiders. All of them added up to something. She was sure of it.

The birds in their chests are fluttering and rising, threatening to choke them. You can almost hear them singing with warbling voices. Halfway across the world, the crows hear it and frown, wondering what's happening. There will be other moments after this, and some of them will get projected on the snow, and some won't get projected anywhere. But before that, there is this moment with the fluttering and the birds and the sudden relentless hope. The whole world sharpens to a single point.

In this moment, Lena and the assistant chef look at each other across the snow. Because of all the scientists, they're both trying to pretend they aren't looking, and it works at first, but then they make eye contact. The assistant chef feels a prickling in her fingers, which start to go numb. Her eyes get starry. She's overwhelmed. The snow melts. The bird in her chest fights to break free and find its partner in song.

There will be other moments, but they're off screen. They're a different script. They are something else entirely.

The snow keeps falling. The projector keeps rolling. Two birds fluttering, two sets of eyes meeting each other, one set hopelessly blue. Nothing has gone wrong just yet. We'll play this part of the tape again. This is the end of the world in Antarctica—the moment before the rest of the story comes to light.

The crows have made a nest to sleep in, just past the archive of brightness. It's made of all the strings that didn't lead anywhere. They still shine. They're still bright enough for the younger crows to have trouble falling asleep, because they're so entranced by the sparkle.

CROW ONE: Are the stories connected to each other?
CROW TWO: They're all the same story.

They're interrupted by Cousin Jesse, clamoring and cawing about the hockey team's latest win. They go off to talk about hockey, about garbage, about how to win their perpetual war with the geese and the seagulls and the pigeons, who are all too close for comfort, all invading their turf.

(It should be noted that the boundaries of the crows' turf are constantly changing.)

Love and love and love and love. Love in the car driving over a mountain, love in the mist, love in a terrible Starbucks, love in a locked room, love in all the rooms that have no locks, love in the moment, love in other moments, love in the terror that everything will change, love in the something else, love in the lovebirds calling to one another, love in the river, love in the sky, love hiding, love in the time of the free market, love in the time of the poetry slam, love and how it works, love and how it doesn't work, love in your veins, love as an anchor dragging you down into the black, love and what the birds see, love and what the birds can't see, love in the automobile industry, love in sacrifice, love in shouting, love in singing, love in the tips of fingers, in words, in the candlelit bar, in the absence of things, in the presence of things. It ends but it never truly stops.

At the end of the world, the shadows of two girls are still holding hands in the dirt-floored cathedral. The girls are still looking up. There is no one else in the room. They are the room. The ceilings are vast. The shadows are shadows of shadows, ghosts of ghosts, so it's hard to know what they're doing. They might be kissing or they might be praying. The sun comes out finally—you can see it through the rafters, reflecting onto the hands—and the shadows darken, sharpening into focus.

Everything happens at once, even if you can't see it.

The goose story, an alternative ending: Eight geese are flying by, a unit, whatever a fleet of geese is. They are honking loudly and gleefully. They are enjoying the sunlight. Eight geese, eight instead of seven, and no one gets left behind anymore.

If you look carefully, one of the geese's wings are scarred, but you can hardly tell through the feathers. You'd hardly know it from the flying. They go on and on, and you follow them, but only with your eyes.

Eight people, eight birds. They never travel alone anymore, and they are always talking, never silent. What a sunset, every night. What an unexpected gift.

The crows have left the archive of brightness for the winter, have left the way it is always sunset there. It isn't that they're abandoning it, it's just that they've been getting overwhelmed and there's a lot of pressure to put meaning into things that don't have it yet. There's a lot of pressure to fix images they aren't sure about just yet. I'm saying "for the winter," but I really just mean "for now." Seasons are relative.

The archive is packed away now, stones covered to slow the process of erosion. The letters from the vulture are carefully preserved, dust and all. (Cousin Jesse can't quite get the sand out of his wings, can't quite shake it off.)

Even as they're flying away, they can't shake the feeling of sunset.

It's dark now, and the archive is all packed away. We need a familiar story to guide us home. All of this weird brightness, birds in the rib cage. You can think of love as something about the spaces in between. The empty park bench, the gaps between your fingers, the places you haven't filled up with something else.

The crows go back to the trees we met them in. It's dark and it's snowing, but it's nothing like the snow in Antarctica. The whole murder is flying from tree to tree, calling out again and again.

Two girls stop, notice the birds, the sky, the tree. They're walking home. There's a catalog somewhere of all of the things they haven't said on this walk. The birds cry out, but from above.

Amid this wild joy, two crows sneak off to be alone.

CROW ONE: So?

CROW TWO: Yes. All the same story. Parts of it, anyway.

CROW ONE: Just—

CROW TWO: What?

The flapping of the murder's wings is getting closer. They might not be alone for long.

CROW ONE: I was hoping for more of an answer. One that explained all the blood.

Pause.

CROW ONE: Was it even worth it?

Another pause.

CROW TWO: Can anyone see us?

CROW ONE: Everyone can see us.

The flapping of wings is getting louder.

CROW TWO: I wonder, though.

Crow Two puts a wing around Crow One and nestles close.
Neither says anything for a long time. The night goes on.

Up ahead, you can just about see the moon. It isn't full, but it might be soon.

The crows fly off to join their murder, black against the sky.
Two girls watch them go.

Acknowledgments

I AM TREMENDOUSLY GRATEFUL to everyone who helped build *An Archive of Brightness*.

Thank you first and foremost to the team at Lanternfish Press—Christine Neulieb, Feliza Casano, and Amanda Thomas—for your care in bringing this novella to life. I've long admired Lanternfish's work and couldn't be more excited to have you as a publisher. Thank you also to everyone who read my submission.

Thank you to Alex for reading the first (very unedited) draft of this manuscript. I very much appreciate the generosity of your time. I couldn't have asked for a kinder first reader or a more constant friend.

So much of this book feels deeply entwined with the year I lived in Maine, as I wrote the first draft in the immediate aftermath. Thank you to my Portland Stage intern cohort for so many things, but most immediately for being willing to plan an imagined escape to Antarctica at the slightest provocation.

Within that cohort, thank you specifically to Emily Golden for her one-act play *Lobstermen in Love,* which is a romantic comedy that doubles as a story of lobsters finding community. It was a joy to work on and an obvious inspiration for Tom and Paul's piece of this story. Thank you also for many years of weekly letters.

Thank you to my parents for being endlessly supportive of me and for sharing links to announcements about this book getting published with all of their friends. Thank you also for lovingly maintaining my childhood book collection, even after a cross-country move.

Thank you most of all to Madison, my most important reader. You always get my references. Thank you for this and everything else, a list truly incalculable.

About the Author

KELSEY SOCHA once wrote and staged a performance piece about lobsters before subsequently quitting theatre to become a librarian. She is originally from Kalamazoo, Michigan, but now lives in Western Massachusetts with her wife and two cats. This is her first book.